THE MAN ON THE WALKWAY

THE MAN ON THE WALKWAY

LESLIE OLDFIELD

First published in Great Britain in 2018 by

Bannister Publications Ltd
118 Saltergate
Chesterfield
Derbyshire S40 1NG

Typeset by Escritor Design, Bournemouth

Printed and bound in Great Britain

Front cover image by Rebekah Ann Keegan
Photograph on back cover by Kate Hallam

Contents

Introduction...vi

A Primal Fear...1

The Horn of Fear..5

The Last Tram...11

A Promise Kept...17

The Night Flyers...23

The Timeless Organ of St Mary's.................35

A Wandering Lady...39

The Unopened Present...................................47

The Lost Carpet Bag.......................................55

A Gothic Tryst..61

A Curious Winter Visitor...............................69

The Man On The Walkway...........................77

The Last Christmas Dinner............................85

The Missing Allotmenteer..............................93

Three Seconds..105

Introduction

The landscape and history of Derbyshire and the Staffordshire Moorlands lends itself to the writing of ghost stories and it is no surprise that authors such as Bram Stoker, Arthur Conan Doyle and Mary Wollstonecraft Shelley have used it as a backdrop for their books and stories.

I have always thought that Edgar Allen Poe was the master of supernatural tales and have been intrigued how he made his short stories extremely thought provoking and more memorable than many longer novels. His influence has guided my own short stories, trusting that the reader will be both entertained, intrigued, and want to return to them again and again to fathom them out.

In the Story, 'The Man on the Walkway', I try to show how a person might feel when he has been diagnosed with Alzheimer's and leave it to the reader to decide what he actually saw. In 'The Lost Carpet Bag', I show how one person copes with a moral dilemma that leads to his eventual downfall.

The backdrop of the Roaches on the Staffordshire Moorlands is the setting for my story, 'The Night Flyers', which concerns the ghosts of three German Airmen. It is based on a real event that happened in May 1941 during the Second World War, when a German Dornier crashed behind the Roaches and all the crew perished. Similarly, 'The

Unopened Present', is based on my experience of discovering in a Peak District churchyard, the grave of a little girl who had died on Christmas Eve. On seeing the grave I thought how difficult it would have been for the child's family to celebrate every subsequent Christmas.

There is a variety of backgrounds to the subjects of my stories. The tale of 'A Wandering Lady', 'The Missing Allotmenteer', 'The Timeless Organ of St Mary's' and 'A Promise Kept' all deal with different types of people and, I hope, will appeal my readers' adventurous minds.

I have taken the liberty of setting one of my stories well outside of the counties of Derbyshire and Staffordshire: 'The Last Christmas Dinner' is set in Hungary. Over the past fifteen years, many people from Central and Eastern Europe have settled in the Peak District and I wanted to show how their Christmas customs differ from those of the native English.

I was born in Buxton and educated at St John's College in Manchester and the University of York. I worked for Stockport Health Authority and Stockport Council. I am a keen gardener and Secretary of Buxton Roman Society and a member of Chatsworth Players, where I recently played Archbishop Cranmer in 'A Man for All Seasons'.

For Jill

A Primal Fear

A HORRIFIC SCREAM REBOUNDED from the walls of the show cave and such was the force of the echo one could have easily thought that it could have detached some of the many stalactites from the cavern's ceiling. The cry of terror was a futile act because no other person was present in the underground darkness and no one could hear anything from outside the cavern's walls.

In Victorian England the Derbyshire spa town of Buxton was a popular destination for visitors looking for something to excite their curiosity, and Alice Fleetwood, a petite and fair-haired young lady from the Black Country town of Wolverhampton, had often suggested to her Aunt Mimi that she would very much like to have a sojourn to the town and see its attractions. Alice, who had been inspired by the likes of women scientists such as Elizabeth Carne and Etheldred Bennett, had a particular interest in geology and was eager to visit the town's famed Poole's Cavern, a show cave that had a particularly wonderful assortment of stalactites and stalagmites.

Alice's benevolent aunt always tried to accommodate her erudite niece's wishes and arranged for the pair of them to travel by train to Buxton in the month of May, in the year of Queen Victoria's golden jubilee in 1887, and to stay at the town's Old Hall Hotel for three nights. Alice's mother duly gave permission for her sister to chaperone her seventeen-year-old daughter to the nearby inland resort and meticulous plans were made for the trip.

Alice and her Aunt Mimi were met by bright sunshine and a tepid wind when they alighted from their train at Buxton's Midland railway station on a Friday morning, and hurried to their nearby hotel so they could unpack their belongings and start to explore the attractions of the town. They had lunch at the Pavilion Gardens and took the waters at the Pump Room in the early evening before attending a choral concert at St John's Church. It was decided between them that they would go shopping on the following Saturday morning and then walk to the Poole's Cavern on the outskirts of the town in the late afternoon and Alice teased her aunt about what little creatures might exist in the cave. However, her aunt was not amused by her levity and told her niece not to talk like a schoolgirl.

Alice was wakened in the night by the sound of her Aunt Mimi vomiting and was concerned for her wellbeing when she appeared extremely pale in the morning. Her aunt, stoically, told her niece not to worry and said that it was probably the ham and cucumber sandwiches that she had eaten yesterday that were responsible for her sickness and said that she needed to rest, and encouraged Alice to go on her own to Poole's Cavern. However, Alice was emphatic she would stay with her aunt for the morning at least to see how things developed.

It seemed around noon that Aunt Mimi was getting better for she was able to eat some of the oxtail soup that had been brought to her, and Alice thought it would be safe to leave her so she could go to the show cave as it would be closed the next day, a Sunday, and they would be travelling back to Wolverhampton on the Monday morning. After getting her things together and kissing her aunt tenderly on the cheek, Alice headed off across the town in the direction of the renowned cavern, and after a forty-minute walk, found herself at the entrance and was astounded to see the vast crowds that were waiting to be guided round the attraction.

Resigning herself to a long wait, she tucked in to the steak pie and lemonade she had purchased on the way to the cave. It took more than three hours for her to become part of a tour party and she was told that her tour group would be the last of that particular day. It transpired that over forty people were in the group and they were led round the cave by a rotund and doddery gentleman in his mid-fifties.

On entering the cavern, Alice was amazed by the sights she saw and was impressed by the guide reciting the names of the famous people who had visited the cavern in earlier times. The gas lamps and candles provided precious little light and as Alice was leaning over a rock to get a better look at the stalagmites, she slipped and hit her head on the cave's hard floor. The fall knocked her completely unconscious and the preoccupied guide failed to notice that one of his party had literally fallen by the wayside.

The final tour group of the day duly trooped out and the grey-haired guide closed the heavy door at the cave entrance and locked it with an enormous iron key; no one could get in or out until it was reopened on the following Monday morning. After about two hours of oblivion, Alice came to her senses and wondered where on earth she was. She rubbed her sore head and was puzzled by the fact that she was in complete darkness; she was fully awake but she could not see a thing.

Suddenly and horrifically it dawned on her where she

3

was, and she realised that she had been encased in the show cave. Her whole body was cold and her spirit of mind was frozen about what she should do. She had nothing to eat or drink and if, god forbid, her aunt had lapsed into delirium, no one would know she was there. A great panic took hold of her and she became mentally crushed by her predicament and involuntarily let out a piercing and terrible scream.

Fear of the dark is probably mankind's most primal fear and unending darkness is extremely difficult to cope with. In prehistoric times it was in total darkness that humans would be predated on by nocturnal and fierce creatures, and humans would make beds in the trees to avoid the attentions of the night-time animal stalkers. Moreover, when one is blind, sounds and senses become more acute and the feeling of terror is increased and this was the case with Alice as she feared she would be stricken with madness if she was not rescued soon.

A burning stinging came to Alice's eyes and at first she thought she was hallucinating, but then she heard a man's voice calling her name and she shouted as loud as she could in the direction of the caller. Soon she saw a man's face lit up by candlelight and started to sob uncontrollably as the man led her to the cave entrance and safety. Fortunately, her aunt had not taken a turn for the worse and had alerted the hotel manager that her niece had not returned from the show cave and he had contacted the local constabulary. Alice duly left Buxton with her Aunt on the following Monday morning and made a pact with herself that she would always sleep with some sort of light on for the rest of her natural life.

The Horn of Fear

T HE CARYNX HORN was used by Celtic tribes to put the fear of death into their enemies, and the sound the instrument made was, by all contemporary accounts, extremely frightening and unearthly. Indeed, the noise emanating from the snake-like instrument could easily have been taken for the roar of a monster by the Iron Age people of Britain and would have undoubtedly caused panic in their ranks.

Maisie and Ryan Fisher were geography teachers and amateur historians from Nottingham who had developed an interest in the archaeological discoveries at the Derbyshire Iron Age fort of Fin Cop in 2011. In particular, they had become fascinated with the uncovering of eight skeletons of women and children at the site. It seemed that the fort had been attacked 2,300 years ago and the bodies of the women and children had been unceremoniously thrown into a ditch. Mysteriously, the skeletons showed no signs of violence other than marks on the feet of all of them, and it had been conjectured by some scholars that the marks could have been caused by them running for their lives over stone strewn ground.

On a misty and inclement early November Sunday morning, Maisie and Ryan parked their SUV at the Monsal Head car park and prepared to ascend to the summit of Fin Cop, which was on the other side of the dale. They had come well prepared for their outing with state of the art outdoor clothing, maps and supplies and were eager and ready to investigate the site of the prehistoric massacre.

They hurriedly descended down the dale and then braced themselves for the steep climb they had to make to get to the site of the Iron Age settlement. Contemptuously ignoring a sign which stated that they were on private property and that trespassers would be prosecuted, they began their arduous ascent to the top.

The task of reaching the summit proved more difficult than they had expected and both of them were completely exhausted when they eventually reached the plateau of Fin Cop where the site of the fort had been discovered. Collapsing on the ground, they swiftly took out bottles from their backpacks and gulped down water to quench their thirsts. It was whilst they were drinking that Maisie thought she heard something. She wasn't quite sure what it was but she didn't recognise it as anything she had heard before.

"Did you hear that?" she promptly asked her husband.

"Hear what?" he replied in a mystified tone of voice.

"I definitely heard something, a very strange sound like that of a wild animal," she insisted.

Her husband said it was probably the wind reverberating round the dale below and began to look at his ordnance survey map to pinpoint the exact spot where the skeletons of the women and children had been found. After resting for a short while and taking their bearings, they advanced to where the fort was situated but were alarmed at how misty it had become for the visibility was very poor and they could barely see two metres in front of them.

Stumbling over a mound, Ryan fell to the ground and as

Maisie went to his assistance a distinct and horrific shriek came from above. It was like the distress call from a huge bird and unnerved both of them as Maisie helped her husband to his feet. Cautiously, they moved towards the prehistoric fort and were just about to enter the site when a horrendous pain was felt in their eardrums, forcing them to cover their ears with their hands in an attempt to shut out the sound which was causing it.

They ran from the fort in the direction they had come from and were relieved to find that the pain in their eardrums gradually subsided and they were able to discuss what had caused it. Ryan suggested they had probably had developed an ear infection which had been exacerbated by the cold and misty weather and that they needed to make an appointment with their respective GPs as soon as they could. Maisie, barely seeing her husband through the mist, nodded her head in agreement and asked if they should give up on investigating the site for that day and head back home. Ryan disagreed and suggested they put their hoods up and make their way back to the Iron Age citadel.

Maisie acquiesced to Ryan's suggestion and they headed once more to the scene of the prehistoric barbarity. Tentatively they made their way back to the site, and were disconcerted to hear what sounded like the discordant notes of a large trumpet or horn. Ryan said it was nothing to worry about but Maisie vehemently disagreed and said the sound was unearthly and worrying and that they should go no further and make their way back down to the dale.

Reluctantly bowing to his wife's wishes, Ryan turned round and retraced his steps and has he did so the horn-like sound increased in volume and the stinging pain in his and Maisie's eardrums returned. Moreover, the mist became totally enveloping and they could not even see their own hands when they put them up to their respective faces.

"Oh my god, please no, please no!" shouted Ryan, and on hearing this Maisie grabbed Ryan's hand and started running in the direction of what she thought was the way they had come to the summit.

They could not see what was in front of them and constantly stumbled and tripped over the uneven and rocky ground as they felt the noise of the horrendous horn increase in intensity. The constant scraping and scuffing made the laces on Maisie's walking boots come undone, and when she cascaded down a ditch her boots and socks came off and she found herself running in just bare feet, hand in hand with her husband away from the ghastly noise.

Totally disorientated and in a state of panic, they were, in fact, not heading the way they had come but rather in the direction of a sheer drop to the east side of their ascent, and were taken so completely by surprise when they felt themselves descending at incredible speed that they were mercifully unaware they were hurtling to oblivion.

The mountain rescue service had been called out to search the area when the landlord of the Monsal Head pub received a telephone call from Maisie's concerned mother asking if he had seen any sign of the young couple. He had previously noticed that a car had been left in the car park for over twenty-four hours and immediately contacted the authorities who called out the local mountain rescue service. The volunteers of the service didn't take long to discover two bodies at the bottom of Fin Cop, and concluding that the two individuals had been dead for quite some time, brought the corpses of Maisie and Ryan in body bags to Monsal Head where they were transferred in a hearse to the local mortuary.

A post mortem was carried out to establish that no foul play had taken place and the coroner subsequently concluded that the deep incisions on Mrs Fisher's feet had probably been caused by her running in bare feet over sharp pointed rocks and that it was safe to assume that the couple had died by misadventure.

The Last Tram

O N THE DOORSTEP of autumn, Leonard Garde went for a late evening stroll in the northern town of Bramington. He had always thought that late August was a good time to reflect on what had happened over the past year and the last twelve months had been a turbulent time for him. For one thing, he had been forced to move home and he found that his new abode was very unsatisfactory for he did not like his new neighbours.

His pondering was disturbed by the last tram to Bramington town centre noisily trundling past him. Observing that many of its passengers were obviously the worse for drink, he tutted to himself about their rude and raucous behaviour and wondered what the world was coming to. In continuing his promenade, he noticed that from the tram stop from where the last tram had recently departed there was a lady sitting on one of the benches provided for waiting tram passengers.

On moving closer, he noticed that she was a very attractive and refined lady of middle age and was baffled as to why she was sitting there and had not boarded the tram. Perhaps, he thought, she did not want to get on because of all the drunken revellers and may have thought another tram would come along soon after. He decided that he would strike up a conversation with her when he passed the tram stop and would dutifully inform her that there would be no more trams due at that particular stop until tomorrow morning.

When he came abreast of her he cleared his throat and wished her a good evening and she responded by wishing him one also. "Madam," he hesitantly began, "are you aware that the tram that has just departed was the last one to do so from this tram stop and that there would not be another one till the morn?"

The lady replied that she was unaware that it was the last one and had decided not to get on because she did not approve of the drunken behaviour of several of its passengers, and had thought that another would come a long before too long. She thanked him for his information and continued to sit on the bench with a serene look on her face and then rustled through her handbag and pulled out a book which she began to read.

Baffled and perturbed by her nonchalant behaviour because the part of Bramington they were in was notorious for the nefarious activities that took place in it, Leonard became concerned for the lady's welfare and was worried that something might happen to her if she stayed at the tram stop on her own.

"Madam," his voice assumed an authoritative air, "this district of the town is infamous for its seedy goings on and is not the sort of place that a lady should be in on her own, particularly in the evening. Indeed, three years ago a woman was found strangled in one of its backstreets and the murderer has not yet been apprehended."

The woman raised her hand in a dismissive manner and told him that she would be alright and that she would read her book for half an hour before walking back to her place of residence.

"Madam," he protested, "I think you are very unwise to walk unaccompanied in this area and I earnestly advise you to hail a passing cab, for I am afraid some footpad or ruffian might assault you on your journey home."

A rueful smile appeared on the woman's face and she said to Leonard that she had no fear whatsoever for her personal safety and that he should proceed with his evening stroll and leave her in peace. Becoming annoyed with her stubbornness, he wondered if she was one of the troublesome suffragettes that he had read about in the newspapers and baited her by saying that he hoped she was not one of those independent minded women who thought men were not needed. She replied by saying that she was not a member of The Women's Political and Social Union but thought that women had the right to vote.

Taking exception to her view he stated that he was totally opposed to women gaining the vote as it would overthrow the natural order of things and bring chaos to the country, adding that women should be at home looking after the nation's children and not going to polling booths. Putting her book down in an emphatic manner she countered him by saying that spinsters like herself had no children to look after, and votes had been given to women in New Zealand in 1904, which had not brought ruin to that country.

Shaking his head he cried, "A mere Dominion, that's all New Zealand is. Great Britain is the Empire's centre and men must be in charge here!"

"Leonard, Leonard, you really are a dinosaur," she ruefully replied.

Astounded and taken aback by how she happened to know his Christian name he demanded to know how she was aware of it. She explained that she resided in the area to where he had recently moved and that her neighbours had informed her of his name. Growing suspicious, as he did not care for his new and obnoxious neighbours, he grumpily asked her what other information about him had they had departed to her. Smugly, she told him that she had found out that his surname was Garde, that he was not married, that his parents were both deceased and that he was in his mid-forties.

Stamping his left foot in anger, Leonard fumed that his new neighbours were idle gossips and that he wished that he had never moved there and would consider relocating. He was then mystified by her reply as she stated to him that he had no choice about moving there and everyone knew things about people there. She added that newcomers to the area always found it difficult to fit in and thought they were still in the other world.

Stunned by what she had said he raised his voice and proclaimed, "Other world, what are you talking about… who are you. What are you?"

"Oh, Leonard, you really are a poor soul and I must insist on walking you home."

Turning to stare directly at the woman's face he became confused, light-headed and unsteady on his feet, and the woman quickly stood up and held him in her arms to support him and presently proceeded to lead him in the direction of home. After about half an hour they came to an area of town he knew well as the tram passed there on the way to the town centre, and passing through some ornate iron gates he found himself standing in front of a stone structure with the mysterious lady pointing to some writing on it. His eyes scrutinised the script and he became incredulous as to what it meant and he read out the words in disbelief.

"Here lies Leonard Garde, the treasured and only son of Gerald and Martha Garde, who was tragically killed in a tram accident on August 10th, 1910, aged 45.
Requeiscat in Pace."

A Promise Kept

DAZZLED BY THE moonlight, three young men stood at the side of the River Wye as it languidly passed through the Derbyshire town of Bakewell. The three friends had recently graduated from Sheffield University, and had agreed to meet up in the picturesque Derbyshire town to have a few beers and console each other as they had not found any work since graduating in early July. The day had been an unusually hot late September day, and they had imbibed a considerable amount of alcohol as they told each other of their dashed hopes and rejections in the job hunting field.

It was in the early 1980s, and with unemployment in Britain approaching four million the three young men were part of the total. Steve Bolton was a politics graduate and Paul Tilson and Mike Woodward were history graduates. They had been close friends since meeting up at their first term at university. It had been good for their morale to meet up again and to laugh, joke and reminisce about their time at college together. Names of lecturers and fellow students were banded about and ridiculed mercilessly and they revelled in renewing their private and esoteric humour.

They each discussed their individual plans of action to find work and Paul and Mike suggested they would attend a post-graduate teaching course at a college in Worcester.

Steve, a dark-haired, tall young man with an aquiline nose, stated that teaching was not for him and he would attempt to rise to be one of the captains of industry and live in a big mansion with several different makes of cars at his disposal. Mike and Paul, both fair-haired and of slim build, mocked his plans and said he was a child of the Thatcher era and wanted to become a yuppie.

Steve, however, was disdainful of their asides and boasted that he would make a success of himself and would not end up like them in some run-down comprehensive school, teaching a load of disruptive school kids and being harangued by their parents for not getting them to achieve good grades at their exams. Paul and Mike, nevertheless, continued to scoff at his ambitious ideas and joked he would probably end up as a liveried doorman at a top London hotel opening doors for the rich and famous.

Having had enough of his mates' ribbing, Steve challenged the two of them to an asseveration. He told them that they should all make an emphatic promise to return to this very spot at midnight in twenty-five years' time to the day. Yes, on September 25th 2006, they would all meet up at this place next to the river and all must clasp hands and promise to make it, whatever their circumstances in the future, and warned them that there would be a curse on any one of them who failed to keep the rendezvous. Paul and Mike at first thought Steve was jesting but seeing the intense look in eyes they realised he was deadly serious and considered the suggestion with earnestness.

Putting out his outstretched right arm, Steve gave his two college friends a stern look and Paul and Mike felt obliged to put out their hands, so all three of them together joined in a solemn pledge and all felt committed to keep it. Maybe, it was the amount of alcohol they had drunk or the ambiance of the flowing river and bright moonlight, but all three of them knew that it was an appointment that they had to keep no matter how their individual lives subsequently developed.

As the years cascaded by, the three friends gradually had less to do with each other, although they had promised that they would always keep in touch. Steve lost contact with the other two altogether and the last they heard about him was that he had found work in Australia with a mining corporation as a financial manager. Moreover, with both Mike and Paul finding partners, getting married and becoming fathers, it meant that their priorities changed and they could no longer live the free and cavalier lives they had led when they were younger. They both worked in the educational field and met up occasionally for a drink, but it was a very tame and boring affair to what it used to be like and without Steve being present it felt as though something was missing.

With the onset of middle age, Mike and Paul started to become nostalgic about their youth and talked often about whether Steve would keep the appointment with them both at Bakewell in a year's time. They teased each other that if he was a success he would definitely attend but if he was on skid row somewhere he would conveniently forget the appointment. The pledge they had made all those years ago seemed like some hazy dream with the passing of the years, but something in their psyches niggled at them and they felt obliged to keep that midnight appointment no matter what their respective partners thought about it as it would appear suspicious to them that their husbands were meeting up at night-time somewhere.

19

Twelve months passed and the cherished day was imminent and, as it was a Monday, Mike and Paul decided to book the Tuesday off from work and catch the bus to Bakewell when they finished work on that particular evening. They met up in the Red Lion pub in the town, and as they downed several pints of beer they started debating whether Steve would keep the rendezvous or get cold feet as he had not been the success he had boasted he would become all those years ago. Paul surmised that they were on a fool's errand as Steve had probably forgotten about the pledge he had made a long time ago and would possibly be on a beach somewhere in Australia with not a thought in the world for the two of them in Bakewell.

They left the Red Lion for the public bar of the Rutland Hotel, and by half past eleven, they downed what was left of their pints in the and started to make their way to the riverside. They had found out that Jane Austen had once stayed at the Rutland Hotel and as they looked back at the hotel, Mike comically remarked that that there was no sense or sensibility in what they were doing as there was no chance whatever that Steve would show up. Paul said that he thought the same but for old friendship's sake they had to be there at midnight.

On reaching the exact spot next to the river where they had made the sacred promise twenty-five years ago, the two of them checked their mobile phones for the right time and saw that it was two minutes to midnight and there seemed to be no sign of their erstwhile friend. However, they were startled to hear a familiar voice behind them as it turned midnight, and turning round they saw Steve, looking gaunt and pale, approaching them. They both noticed that he didn't seem to have changed much and his hair had not a thread of grey in at all. They greeted him enthusiastically but he seemed uncharacteristically laconic and evaded any of their questions. In an instant a flash of light appeared in the sky and Mike and Paul looked up to see what it was and when they looked down again they noticed that Steve had vanished. Both of them were perplexed as to where he had gone and were even more puzzled when he never appeared again. For days afterwards they dwelled on why he had only made a transient appearance with them, and thought it was the height of ignorance to have disappeared like that without saying a proper goodbye to either of them after all those years, especially with both of them going out of their way to keep the appointment that he had arranged.

In the ensuing days Mike, nonplussed by Steve's behaviour, became very curious about what had occurred and made it his business to find out where on the planet he was living and what exactly he was doing. He checked Facebook, voting registers, marriage registers and old newspaper records he could find online and didn't leave a stone unturned, and eventually he found a picture in a 1987 Melbourne newspaper that staggered, bewildered and numbed him. The picture in the newspaper was clearly that of his friend and the caption under it stated that a young Britain working as a financial consultant to a mining company had been killed in a head-on collision with another car in the early hours of September 25th, 1987.

The Night Flyers

THE BLAZING INFERNO below made the perplex front of the German bomber plane glisten like a chandelier as Major Dietrich Baum gave himself an imaginary pat on the back, and the metaphorical cream could be clearly seen on his whiskers as he thought that he and his crew had truly completed the object of their mission.

From 1938 onwards, when he bombed Barcelona in the Spanish Civil War, his bombing missions had all gone without many problems. He was lucky, for he had not taken part in the daylight campaign against Britain in the summer of 1940, where the Luftwaffe had taken heavy losses, and he had just come back from training school to rejoin his Heinkel squadron and the night-time campaign against Great Britain in the autumn.

He and his three crew members looked in awe at the conflagration they had contributed to at the Liverpool dockyards underneath them. All had gone well so far, as the outbound journey had been uneventful and the British anti-aircraft gunners had again misjudged the height of the raiding planes as they could see the shells exploding well below them.

The shell bursts gave a feeling of defiance to the people of Liverpool but gave no serious worries to the crews of the Heinkel 111s and Junkers 88s who had been unleashing their deadly and destructive presents on the city for most of the clear and tepid May night.

Baum had been flying with the same bunch now for six months: Lt Neuman, the navigator; Schnieder, the wireless operator, and Eisner, the tail gunner. There was much gossip amongst the flyers of the squadron about new radar devices the British were using that could detect enemy planes at night and allow the British pilots to locate them. It was with this in mind that the entire crew were wary and apprehensive about the return journey. Baum ordered Eisner to be especially vigilant as the British would have had plenty of time to have taken off and place themselves on the probable trajectory of the homebound marauders.

Waiting on the outskirts of Manchester, like an owl waiting for a mouse to make a slight movement that would give its position away to a predator, was an RAF Boulton Paul Defiant two-seater night fighter. The alert pilot thought he saw a black object amongst the clouds and changed his direction to intercept whatever it was.

Unbeknown to Major Baum was the fact that the campaign against Britain was about to be eased and two thirds of the bomber squadrons, including Baum's, were to be transferred to the east. Hitler had decided to attack the Soviet Union, and like Napoleon before him, was pretending to launch an invasion of England in order to deceive the Russians.

Also unbeknown to the German pilot and crew was the fact that they would not be taking any part in that colossal struggle in the east at all. The crew were all individually thinking about what they would be doing in two days' time when they were all on leave. Baum would visit Zandvoort to get some sea air; Lt Neuman would visit Breda to buy a present for his mother's forthcoming birthday; Schnieder and Eisner would visit Amsterdam together and they would sample both the Dutch beer and ladies. Indeed, Eisner could almost smell the hoppy fragrance of a freshly opened bottle of Amstel beer when it was dramatically and horrifically replaced by that of cordite and petrol fumes.

The starboard wing had been ripped apart by bullet fire and was well alight. Major Baum tried desperately to stabilise the plane, but instinctively knew the aircraft was doomed. He ordered Schnieder to radio that the crew were about to bail out and told Eisner to get out first. He then told Schnieder to follow him.

The stricken Heinkel, with one wing engulfed in flames, was flying over the Staffordshire town of Leek. Baum thought he was flying at an altitude of 3,000 metres as Schnieder was just about to follow Eisner out of the plane who had parachuted seconds before. In fact, his instruments were wrong and, unfortunately for them all, the grim, formidable and skulking Roaches were directly in front of them.

As unknowingly as a sparrow flying into the pane of a greenhouse, the aerial warhorse hit the side of the moorland hillside with a deafening crash and the young German airmen became three more victims of Hitler's mad war.

Pauline Simmett, a nine-year-old farmer's daughter, had been looking out of her bedroom window when she witnessed a moving flame explode into the ground just upland from the farmhouse where she and her family lived. She fell back in shock and frantically called out to her mother.

Her mother rushed into the room to check on her and tenderly embraced the young girl. "Mummy, mummy, what is it," she called out to her mother.

"It's a German plane, my love," she said assuredly and added, "serves them right," in a sanctimonious tone, for in the March of that year a young butcher had been killed in Leek's Monk Street caused by a German Bomber discarding its load and Mrs Simmett was not in the mood for compassion. Pauline turned away from her mother and looked again at the burning debris on the moors and thought it reminded her of a November 5th bonfire.

"Can we go and see the wreckage tomorrow?" she asked eagerly of her mother.

"I suppose so," her mother replied, "but I bet half the town of Leek and Quarnford will be there as well."

The next day, Pauline and her mother walked briskly in the morning sunshine to where the plane had foundered. The scene awaiting them there was not as Pauline had imagined it would be. For a start, the crash scene had been completely sealed off by the Leek Homeguard and the three frizzled bodies of the Germans had been covered with sheets by the soldiers and were waiting to be taken away. Pauline gasped when she glimpsed a blackened foot protruding from one of the sheets with an exposed ankle bone clearly visible. In the months that followed, Pauline would be troubled by visions when she walked the moors on her own for she thought she saw three black and skulking figures standing on the Roaches.

Many years after the war had ended Pauline would ramble around the mysterious rocks and would occasionally, she thought, see the same three blackened individuals. Whenever she walked near the old crash site, Pauline would become frileuse. The French word has no direct translation in the English Language and means always feeling cold whatever the weather or situation. Even on a hot, glorious

August afternoon with the heather looking stunning on the moors, she would feel cold when she went near the spot where the bodies had been covered with sheets in 1941.

Pauline would later marry a Frenchman and live in the beautiful city of Rouen for over twenty years, but when the marriage turned sour she divorced her husband and moved back to her hometown in the 1990s. However, even after a gap of many years, she would still see the three apparitions and shiver with cold when she went anywhere near the old plane's final resting place.

The sunshine sparkled on the metallic green on the modernised version of the classic Volkswagen Beetle as it passed out of Buxton and ascended to the Staffordshire moorlands like a gliding bird. Inside the car were three young women, who were all students at Durham University, and had just been camping near Bakewell. Emily, who had just spent part of her gap year in East Arica, remarked how curiously similar the landscape was to Kenya and she almost imagined the rolling green hillsides to be inhabited by zebras and wildebeest.

Emily and her two friends, Lauren and Sophie, were impatient to see the gritstone escarpment guarding the entrance to the Peak District known as the Roaches, and they were not disappointed when it came into their view with Lauren exclaiming, "It's where you would expect a Witches' Coven to meet," and Sophie also commented it looked like an Aboriginal's sacred meeting place. Indeed, they were all genuinely impressed with the primal rock formation and thought it would be a great place for a spot of random, wild camping and they spontaneously agreed to set up camp there in the early evening. They would first, however, visit Leek before they came back with all they needed to spend a very special night there.

Leek was their destination because Sophie, a second-year history student, had a special interest in the place. Her father was from Trinidad, and as a girl he had talked to her many times about the great black slave leader, Toussaint L'Ouverture. She became a lover of all things historical and especially of black Caribbean history. In fact, she was working on a dissertation about the life of Toussaint and she was aware that Leek had a curious and important part in it, for it was here that General Brunet, the man who had tricked and captured the black icon, had served his parole after being captured by the British.

From 1803 to 1812, Leek served as parole town for captured French soldiers and sailors of high rank and Brunet lived quite a comfortable life as a prisoner there. He was a Freemason and would frequent the 'Reunion Desiree' at the Red Lion in the market square, and was allowed to travel out of the town and make regular trips to Buxton to take the waters and drink brandy at the town's Sun Inn.

Standing in the market square of Leek, Sophie took stock of the situation and felt angry that whilst Brunet had had a comfortable 'imprisonment', Toussaint, the man he had entrapped, suffered a cruel, lingering and deliberate death in a cold damp dungeon in the Doubs area of eastern France. Whilst she pondered Toussaint's unhappy fate her two friends looked around and thought Leek a pleasant and homely town.

After visiting the memorial to the French servicemen, who were buried in the grounds of St Edward the Confessor's church, they went to have a look at the quintessentially gothic Nicholson Institute where the town's library was based. Later on as they ambled round the town, they were amused and intrigued by a pub called The Wilkes' Head, in memory of John Wilkes, an eighteenth-century democratic campaigner who was popular with American revolutionaries. He ruffled the feathers of King George III with his critical pamphlets and was tried for seditious libel. Sophie also remarked to the other two women that John Wilkes Booth, the man who had assassinated Abraham Lincoln, was named after him.

The threesome continued to roam the streets of the picturesque market town for most of the afternoon until Emily spotted a quaint old café on Derby Street and suggested they all have tea and scones there. They imperiously entered the café and sat together at a window table and beckoned over a young teenage waitress to serve them.

Whilst waiting for their scones, Sophie started to show off her knowledge of French, which she had been learning for the last two years, with witticisms about Leek and elsewhere. Unbeknown to her and the other two, there was an elderly lady sitting behind them in the café who could speak far better French than any of them and who became alarmed when she gathered from the students' conversation that they were going to camp on the Roaches that night, the exact anniversary of the German Plane crash of 1941, for the grey-haired lady was Pauline Simmett.

Fearful of what might happen to the young women on the moors that night with the three menacing spectres still haunting the crash site, Pauline decided she had to do something to put them off going there. She thought that they would only laugh and sneer at her if she told them about the ghosts of the German airmen so decided, noting that one of them could speak good French, that she would

29

warn them in a cryptic way. Presently, she stood up, walked over to their table and stared directly at Sophie and roared, "Les Maudits!" Afterwards she just turned her back on the students and walked briskly out of the café without a backward glance.

The three women looked gobsmacked and Lauren blurted out, "Nut job, she's a complete nut job." Emily and Sophie nodded in agreement and the three went on to joke about the inbreeding in rural areas as a way of making light of the incident. Lauren asked Sophie what the expression, *Les Maudits* meant, but for all her knowledge of French Sophie could not recall what it was. After paying the bill, the three of them headed for the supermarket to buy the supplies for the forthcoming evening and Emily presciently stated that it was going to be one hell of a night.

Bread, butter, sausages, tomatoes, burgers and crates of Belgian lager were loaded in to the boot of the Volkswagen before the three students headed off in the direction of the Roaches. They arrived at their destination at just after 6pm by way of an old, winding and uneven country lane and quickly erected their blue-coloured tent on a sloping valley between Hen Cloud and Ramshaw Rocks, about 90 metres away from where they had parked their car.

After sorting out the groundsheets and sleeping bags they set up a barbecue and began cooking immediately, and the smell of frying sausages, burgers and onions wafted over the moors and made them all hungry. It was a beautiful May evening and kestrels could be seen hovering in the distance as the students prepared to tuck into their food. They made merry together and were enthralled as a stunning Staffordshire sunset gave an ethereal glow to the Roaches.

As the evening went on, the girls began to talk about boys

30

and past relationships and Emily started to become quite scathing about members of the opposite sex. She was a true hoyden and boasted she could out-booze, out-swear and out-sex any man on the planet, and the other two were amused at her outbursts and giggled as she continued to denigrate males. They were unaware, however, as they chatted and laughed that three dark spectres, the ones that Pauline had tried to warn them about, were watching their every move from behind some rocks nearby.

When it grew dark the mood of the rural soiree began to change as the young women became increasingly inebriated and, though the barbecue was still very hot, they stated to feel very cold and clammy. Indeed, the atmosphere became sombre and serious as Lauren and Sophie thought they saw men on the hills approaching their camp and became agitated as the figures suddenly disappeared. Emily accused the other two of being wimps and, full of bravado, said she would walk over to where they had seen the mysterious walkers and relieve herself there.

She gave a cheeky smile to the other two as she headed off in the direction of the sighting and started to hum a tune when she was about 40 metres away from the camp site. When she reached the place where the figures had been seen she defiantly pulled down her denim shorts, squatted and started to urinate. Just as she was about to pull up her pants she felt something cold and hard touch her left shoulder. She turned round immediately and went into a state of shock as she saw a huge, black and misshaped hand grasping her.

She rose frantically and began screaming hysterically as she ran back to where the two other girls were. Sophie grabbed hold of her as she reached the camp and shook her with some force. "What stuff have you taking recently?"

she demanded of Emily. Again she asked, "What have you been taking, tell me!"

"Nothing," simpered Emily, "Nothing."

Sophie was just about to shake her again when she clearly saw three blackened, disfigured and horrific figures approaching from behind Emily's back. "Oh my god," she exclaimed as she suddenly remembered what *Les Maudits* meant in English: The Damned! "Run for the car, everybody," she shouted at the top of her voice.

She grabbed Emily, and with Lauren close behind, they ran as fast as they possibly could to the Volkswagen parked just ahead of them. Lauren could sense the three spectres chasing and gaining ground on them. Sophie reached for the car keys in her pocket and prayed that the car would start straight away.

Out of breath and out of their minds with terror they reached the car and jumped in. Lauren and Emily were relieved when they heard the car engine start up as Sophie turned the ignition key. The Beetle lurched forward and Sophie accelerated and drove recklessly down the old, uneven and bumpy lane. She had consumed great deal of alcohol during the evening and was in no fit state to drive a vehicle at all. Moreover, she had forgotten that at the sharp bend ahead stood a formidable looking sycamore tree and that even a sober driver would have difficulty taking the corner at speed.

Pauline Simmett was at that moment, coincidentally, looking out of the same bedroom window that she had seen the German plane crash on that dreadful night in 1941. As she looked out now she was startled when she heard a tremendous thud and explosion and saw a huge ball of flames on the hillside, realising at once it was virtually at the same spot as the Heinkel had crashed all those years before and she wondered what had been the cause of it.

In the autumn of the same year, on a cold and frosty day at a time between twilight and darkness that the French call, *Entrée chien et loup* (The time between dog and wolf), Pauline was walking near the site of the old plane crash when she suddenly felt clammy and nervous and knew instinctively that the spectres were in the vicinity. She looked up at the hillside and saw not the usual three apparitions but six. The spectres were split up into couples and seemed to be embracing each other. From thence onwards she always saw six figures on the moors and her sense of coldness became more intense.

The Timeless Organ of St Mary's

DURING THE TRAUMATIC and tragic years of the First World War very few churches were built in Britain, but one of the exceptions was the beautiful Arts and Crafts church of St Mary's the Virgin in Buxton Spa, in the county of Derbyshire. Had the church been built in a more picturesque part of the town, it would have been considered one of the gems of the area but its position next to a main road and a backdrop of prosaic dwellings had caused it to be underrated and overlooked by visitors and townspeople alike.

However, when Albert Jenkins came to live in the town in the early 1990s he was at once awestruck by the charms of the church with its eyebrow dormer windows, and recognised it at once as being inspired by the early twentieth-century Art and Craft movement and felt an instant affinity with it. Albert had just moved from Salisbury to work in Buxton's town planning office, and as a practising Anglican, decided that he would choose to worship at St Mary's. In Salisbury he had been a volunteer under organist at the cathedral and had learnt some interesting theories concerning church organs from the celebrated but eccentric organ maestro, Archibald Dyson.

Dyson had informed Albert that organ music played inside a church edifice could penetrate the souls of people that no other type of music could. It was for this reason, its ability to lift people's spirits heavenward, that organs had been an integral part of churches since the 1400s. He gave an example of this to him when only the two of them were present at twenty minutes to midnight in the vast and magnificent Salisbury Cathedral on a cold November evening. Dyson played the organ at maximum volume, a thing he could never had done with a congregation present, and showed to Albert how the music could never sound as loud with people present because their bodies would absorb the sound waves and dull the effect. Moreover, he expounded the view to him that church buildings could store the same sound waves and miraculous things could be possible because of it.

Albert was intrigued by what Dyson had told him, and when he offered his services to St Mary's as an assistant organist he hoped he would be able to test out some of the ideas that Dyson had hinted at and this was enhanced by his finding out that the organ at St Mary's predated the building itself. The organ, he discovered, had come from the church of St James the Greater, which had been situated on Bath Road in the town. The church had closed in 1953 and was subsequently demolished and its Victorian organ, to the delight of its churchgoers, was transferred to St Mary's.

When the official organist was on holiday or unavailable Albert relished the chance to play the wonderful instrument and felt the full joy of his belief in Jesus when he heard the congregation singing along to the hymns he was playing. Surely, he thought, Dyson had been right when he said that organ music could envelop the soul of its listeners and perhaps miracles were indeed possible.

Suddenly, when playing the organ at a young couple's

wedding one glorious Saturday afternoon in May, a flash of an idea came into his head and he longed to have a chance to explore it. Dyson had stated to him that church music could capture a moment and that music would always be timeless, particularly if it was performed at a scene of great joy and happiness. Yes, he reflected, that could very well be true because doesn't everyone recall certain events when they hear a particular tune or melody? Indeed, most people have a favourite record that conjures up images in their mind when they hear it on the radio or in a supermarket. Isn't that, he propounded, why Christmas carols have so much resonance for people, even non-Christians, because they bring back to them the spirit of Christmases of their childhood and former times?

Albert decided that he would, on the premise of practising hymns he hadn't played for a long time, play the organ at maximum volume when the church was completely empty and he realised that the coming Monday evening would the present the ideal chance he had been waiting for. Duly, he unlocked the church at nine o'clock and made his way to the organ seat. He had recently discovered one of the old hymn books of St James the Greater and thought that some of the lesser known hymns of that book would be perfect to test out his wondrous theory.

Playing at full throttle he gave the 1874 organ its head and was amazed at the acoustics of the church and he felt that his soul was bursting with joy as he manipulated the organ keys. The third hymn he played was one that was particularly popular at weddings during the Great War and he strangely thought he heard voices singing along to it when he was halfway through playing it and this completely mystified him, for he was certain he had locked the church doors when he had entered earlier and there was no chance that any passers-by could have gained access.

As he continued to play the hymn, he became aware that the voices were becoming louder. He was totally bemused and a feeling of anxiety gripped him as he desisted from touching the keyboard. Nevertheless, the voices persisted in singing the hymn and a frisson of fear shot through his entire body. Involuntarily, he stood up and nervously walked to where he could see a full view of the church. A few steps later, an incredible sight confronted him and he fell to his knees when he saw the amazing vision of a wedding of a soldier in First World War army uniform standing next to a serene and beautiful bride who looked the picture of happiness as a large congregation behind them were singing the hymn at the top of their voices.

A Wandering Lady

A BLAST OF ICY cold December air hit Andrew Porter as he left the crowded pub he had been drinking in for the last two hours. Fed up with noise and being squashed like a sardine in a damaged tin, he had decided that, in spite of the freezing conditions outside, he needed to take a rain check. He had been in the Derbyshire town of Buxton for less than twenty-four hours but was already missing the comparatively balmy conditions of his north London home.

He had been chosen by his electronics firm, Ensac Ltd, to attend the 'Pathways for Electronics' conference as a representative of the company in Buxton and was suspicious why he, as a middle manager, had been put forward to attend ahead of any senior manager. He quickly realised, when he alighted from the train at Buxton station and was met by snow and a biting wind, that his suspicions were entirely justified. Cynically, he thought to himself, that if the conference had taken place in July he most certainly wouldn't have been the appointee and, no doubt, a higher-up would have grabbed the gig.

The conference had been a rather tiresome experience and mostly covered areas which he knew about already. The usual bunch of mercenary academics, secretly paid by electronics companies to back their products were there, and the usual married company representatives were there, he ruefully reflected. Porter, a bachelor in his mid- thirties, always thought it was both ironic and hypocritical that most of the married representatives ended up in bed with other married representatives at their respective hotels. The work conference, it seemed, was a good cover for their sexual shenanigans.

When the conference had ended on the Thursday evening, Porter looked forward to sampling the ales in the local hostelries and made sure he declined any offers of going out drinking with any other of the attendees. One thing he didn't want, as he combed his dark brown curly hair in his hotel room, was someone boring him to death with what had been said at the conference. No, he would enjoy his own company and get merrily drunk in the snow-covered taverns of the town.

One of the friendly Hungarian waiters in the hotel had informed him that the best pubs were on the market place in the town, and when Porter had finished his grooming – putting on his most expensive aftershave just in case he got lucky – he made his way from the imposing and ornate Victorian hotel he was staying in to an area of the town he had been recommended to go to.

Snowflakes greeted him as he descended the hotel steps, and as he looked out at the town on that glacial evening he cheerfully thought that it was like someone had spilt a huge tin of white gloss paint over it. Head down against the wind, he headed upwards to the town's market place and scuttled into the first pub he came upon; he didn't even bother to take note of the name of it. All that concerned him was getting in from the Siberian conditions and having some of the 'Sovereign alchemist' that turns life's leaden metal into gold.

That line from the medieval Persian poem 'The Rubaiyat of Omar Khayyam' had always stuck in Porter's mind since he had first read it at the tender age of seventeen. Yes, he said to himself, after all that boring bunkum at the conference he needed some beers inside him to transmute to a different state of mind.

He had stood quite happily at the bar for his first three pints of cask real ale but, gradually, the pub had started to fill up with refugees from office Christmas parties that had been taking place elsewhere. Men and women with red Santa hats in various stage of inebriation crowded round the bar eager to imbibe more alcohol. Most of the women, who wore black or purple mini-skirts, gave him engaging smiles when they gently shoved him out of the way to get served. At first, he enjoyed the jovial atmosphere which the party goers brought into the ale house, but as the numbers increased, and their drunken behaviour worsened, he decided that it was time to leave. Anyhow, he thought, he had supped enough beer and did not want to have too much of a hangover in the morning for he had to catch an early train back to the metropolis.

On leaving the bar, he decided that he would head back to his hotel by way of an area of the town called 'The Slopes', for it would be quicker and would afford him a splendid view of the spa town in its winter vestments. The fresh cold air heightened his senses, and as he walked on the tiered and wooded Slopes he noticed what appeared to be a war memorial at the centre of it. He was just about to turn sideways and walk in the direction of the snow-covered monument when he caught a glimpse of something white moving on his right.

He turned round briskly to see what it was, and was

41

concerned that he might have been followed onto the landscaped area by some local thug who was looking for someone to rob to supplement his Christmas finances. In front of him, however, was no home-grown hooligan but a young, stunningly attractive woman with shoulder-length, light brown hair, who appeared to be dressed in nothing more than a whitish, diaphanous gown. It was an astonishing sight to behold and he was instantly worried for her welfare. Assuming that she was a young Christmas reveller who had had too much to drink and had lost her way, he called out to her, "Are you alright?"

She did not appear to hear his call and carried on walking away from him in a sort of lilting walk that made him come to the reluctant conclusion that she was high on some sort of recreational drug and, he was alarmed to apprise, she was completely barefoot. He quickened his pace to reach her and felt sure that he had to do something to help her, for on such a freezing night as this one she was in danger of dying from hypothermia.

In coming alongside her, he was amazed to find that she did not seem to be feeling the effects of the bitterly cold night at all. She was not shivering and her teeth were not chattering and, moreover, her countenance gave no sign of distress. To all intents and purposes, he reflected, she could have looked no different if she had been taking the same walk on a balmy, warm summer evening. It was mystifying and he didn't know what to do for the best.

Reaching in his trouser pocket for his smart phone, he contemplated calling the police and informing them that there was a young woman, insufficiently dressed for the cold, wandering about the town and that it would be advisable for them to send some officers to check her out.

Instantly, he realised, that the police would not consider that information important as at that festive time of the year there would be probably many young women insufficiently dressed for the conditions carousing around the streets.

"Are you alright?" he repeated again in an exasperated voice. Again, she acted as though he was not there and walked on in a distracted state of mind. "You need to get a taxi and get home as soon as possible or you will catch your death of cold," he implored her, and nobly told her that he would give her the money for the taxi if she did not have any on her as he alarmingly became aware that she was carrying no bag or purse on her person.

All of a sudden she stopped in her tracks, turned, stared directly at him and gave a wistful smile. She then raised her arm up in a theatrical manner and spoke the words, "*Dulce bellum inexpertis*". Dumbfounded by what he recognised as a Latin expression he took a step backwards and came to the conclusion that she was off her head and reached for his phone to call a taxi to take her home and to safety.

As he reached for his phone, he became aware that she was walking from him and heading back to the centre of The Slopes, and hurriedly dialled a local taxi company asking them to send a car to the area as quickly as they could. After the taxi firm informed him that they would send one in the next five minutes he turned to see where she had gone and was shocked to see that she had disappeared. Briskly walking in the last direction he had seen her go, he was nonplussed to see no sign of her and could not for the life of him figure out where she had gone.

After searching for her everywhere for the next few minutes and not finding any sign of her, he lifted his head disconsolately and gave out a sigh. He was just about to search the area again when he became aware of flashing lights and the hooting of a car horn and realised that the taxi he had called for her was beckoning him. Abandoning his pursuit of the elusive lady, he trudged through the snow to the waiting taxi below. The taxi driver gave him a disdainful look after he explained what had happened and drove off towards the town's market place. Before going back to the hotel he decided to give the area one more going over because he was concerned that the woman might have fallen. He searched the war memorial area thoroughly and checked every bench and hollow before he became assured that she was no longer on The Slopes.

The following morning, he breakfasted early and speedily packed his belongings ready to catch the early train to London. However, when he exited the hotel a sudden yearning came over to him to revisit The Slopes. Somehow, he felt there was something he had missed but he could not quite put his finger on it. Realising he had no more than ten minutes to spare before he caught his train, he hurried off in the direction of the area he had last seen the mysterious wandering lady.

It was only just becoming dawn but, in the half-light, he was sure he noticed something different about the war memorial as he glanced at it in passing. Yes, astonishingly, it was not the same as he had seen it the night before because a statue of a human adorned the front of it and he was absolutely sure that one was not there the previous evening. Brimming with curiosity, he went over to the front of the memorial and inspected the statue at its van.

A frisson went through his body like a bolt of lightning going through a church spire as he registered that the statue was that of a beautiful young woman in a see-through gown who looked a dead ringer for the lady he had tried to help the night before. He became more intrigued when he noticed that the Latin inscription, *Pro Patria*, was written above her. A confounded expression came over him as he turned around and walked back in the direction of the train station. Had he had too much to drink the preceding night or had some sort of hallucinatory drug being surreptitiously dropped into his pint pot by a mischievous reveller?

Hours later, when the train he was on was nearing Euston station, an inspirational idea came to him and made him sit up in his seat. Maybe, the lady was a figment of his imagination or maybe she was a living conscience. Maybe, the incongruously erotic-looking young woman attached to the war memorial was tired of her role of placating the living. Tired of giving female blessing to the actuality of war; tired of giving the impression that all those young men reposed in peace when in actual fact they, in the prime of their manhood, had been denied the joys of love and romance from the moment they had fallen and just had a cold blanket of soil for their bodily comfort. Yes, he concluded, remembering the Latin he had been taught at school, war is only tolerable to those who have never experienced its horrors.

The Unopened Present

IT WAS TEN days before Christmas and the Rainow family had taken the carefully stored Christmas decorations down from the loft. All was ready for Mr Rainow when he came back from the town market with the Christmas tree.

It was 1908, and the Rainow family had been living in the Derbyshire town of Belper for the last five years after moving from the Ardwick area of Manchester. Mr Rainow had secured a job at the town's North Mill as an assistant manager and was happy that he could afford to give his four children the full trappings of a British Christmas.

Several years before, times had been hard for him and he had felt guilty that he could not give his wife and children all the essentials of a festive Christmas. However, austerity was a thing of the past for them now and he was determined to make the coming yuletide one of the best they had ever had.

His family consisted of his wife, Elizabeth, and his four daughters who went by the names of Margaret, Anne, Alice and Helen. Margaret, at ten years old, was the eldest and was, by far, the most adventurous of the four girls. Her mother would often say that she should have been born a boy and to a large extent her father treated her as an honorary boy.

Having no son to accompany him in his hobbies and

pursuits he would take his beloved Maggie with him as a substitute. She was taught how to swim by him and would go for long cycle rides with her father whilst her other three sisters stayed at home with their mother learning how to sew and playing with their respective dolls.

In the run-up to Christmas, the younger girls had pestered their father with requests to have more dolls and doll houses delivered to them by Father Christmas on the holy day. But Maggie, on the other hand, who did not any longer believe in the white-bearded man, had asked her father to buy her a cricket bat and fishing rod for Christmas.

When he eventually came back from Belper's market with the evergreen fir tree, his wife and four children were eager and excited and couldn't wait to start decorating it. As he entered the front door of the grey stoned terraced house, all the four girls rushed towards him and hugged and embraced him in turns. It was a scene of supreme family happiness and their joyful cries could be heard by passers-by on the street outside.

The girls helped their mother put all the usual decorations on the tree. There were beautiful coloured baubles, red and white candles, gold and silver tinsel, and charming, huge red bows. Finally, the mother lifted the youngest child, Helen, to the top of the tree to put the cherubic angel on the summit. There was also one particular ritual to carry out before all the family could sing the German Christmas hymn 'Tannenbaum' around the fully dressed tree.

This ritual was something special to the Rainow family and comprised of bringing an unopened present down from the loft to put under the Christmas tree. Maggie was sent by her mother to bring it down and place it gently under the newly adorned tree. Maggie hated going up the ladder to go into the dark and gloomy loft to retrieve the present but she was an obedient child and always did what her parents told her to do.

The unopened present had a very sad and special significance to Elizabeth and she always welled up with tears when it was brought down and put under the Christmas fir tree. The present had been intended for her beloved and fondly remembered sister, Charlotte, at a Christmas over thirty years ago. Charlotte had always been a sickly child and suffered from all sorts of ailments but she had had a sweet and engaging character and had been greatly loved by her parents and her brothers and sisters.

At that fateful Christmas years before, she had taken a turn for the worse and had started to breath with great difficulty. A doctor had been brought to the abode on the night of Christmas Eve and after examining the young girl had left some medicine for her to take. However, on the following Christmas morning no sounds were heard from the bedroom where Charlotte slept. Charlotte loved Christmas and in previous times had awakened early and caused a cacophony in rushing downstairs to open her presents under the Yule tree.

Charlotte's parents, with great trepidation, had entered her room to discover that their greatest fear had been realised. Charlotte had passed on during the course of the night and their precious daughter laid stiff and cold in her bed. From that Christmas on, her parents had always put her unopened present under the family Christmas tree. Elizabeth's father had died three years after Charlotte and her mother had passed away some twelve years later. On her deathbed she had made her eldest child, Elizabeth, promise that at every Christmas she would continue the practice of putting Charlotte's unwrapped present under the family Christmas tree and Elizabeth had dutifully carried out her wishes.

When Maggie brought the sacred unopened gift into the parlour she handed it reverentially to her mother who solemnly placed it at the bottom of the beautifully decorated Christmas tree. Then, with the coal fire roaring in the hearth and giving the room an orange glow, they all sang 'Tannenbaum' around the candle-lit tree.

O Christmas Tree, O Christmas Tree
Your branches green delight us!
They are green when summer days are bright,
They are green when winter snow is white
O Christmas Tree, O Christmas Tree
Your branches green delight us!

The following days for Maggie, like all children at this special time of year, seemed to go very slowly and it seemed like an eternity to her before she was sitting up on her bed on Christmas Eve in a state of high expectation. It was so cold outside that her bedroom window had completely frozen over and she could not tell if there was snow on the ground outside. While she was contemplating what would be in her presents under the Christmas tree a mischievous thought came into her head.

From seemingly out of nowhere, she had suddenly decided that she would creep down the stairs in the middle of the night whilst her parents and sisters were fast asleep. She further decided that she would take with her scissors and glue and carefully open the unopened present that was always put under the Yule tree every year by her mother.

It was as though she felt she had a compulsion to do it, though it was totally against her natural behaviour for she always obeyed her parent's instructions as she was in no way a recalcitrant child.

She slowly and carefully descended the stairs and then gently opened the parlour door. She made a concerted effort to be as quiet as possible and listened intently for any noise emanating from upstairs. She saw the Christmas tree in the dim light given off by the dampened down but still glowing fire. She also could make out the famous present with its now faded wrapping paper. She tiptoed to it and began the task of using the scissors to carefully unwrap it. She was very tense and nervous and dreaded being caught by her father or mother.

Finally, she removed all the paper and was able to open the box containing the unknown present which had been intended for her mother's dead sister. She hesitantly removed the box's lid and winced with horror when she thought she saw a dead creature looking at her. After a moment she realised that it was not a dead animal but a finely made toy dog with soft imitation fur. She briefly felt relieved and then she heard the parlour door creak open and was mortified and fearful that her errand had been heard by her parents and that she would have to face their anger and disapproval.

She reluctantly turned her head expecting to see either her mother's or father's reproachful eyes looking at her, but was aghast to see a young girl with spectral light behind and all around her standing there. The little girl had very long fair hair and a gaunt and wan complexion. She also had eyes which appeared to be bloodshot and her appearance terrified Maggie. This state of terror increased when she realised that the apparition was walking straight towards her.

Maggie couldn't bear to watch. She closed her eyes and went in to a state of 'tonic immobility': the name given to what a rabbit does as a last resort measure to stop a predator killing it. She was completely still and not giving off any sound at all. She expected at any moment to receive a fatal assault from the spectre and regretted bitterly that she had the temerity to creep downstairs and open the sacred present.

Instead of the blow she expected she was astonished and relieved to hear a mellifluous voice address her. She heard the words "Thank you" and suddenly became able to open her eyes and then clearly saw the little girl gently take the toy dog out of the box and cradle it her arms. The girl then turned and walked back towards the door carrying the dog with her. When she reached the door the spectral light disappeared and she could be seen no more.

Maggie drew in a deep breath and began quickly with the scissors and the glue to put the wrapping paper back on the present and place it back as it was before. Following such an extraordinary ordeal she did not know where she found the savoir faire to complete this task, and when she had accomplished it she went as quietly as a mouse back up the stairs and into her bedroom. She had never been as happy to rest her head on her pillow and surprisingly went straight to sleep.

On the following Christmas morning, she woke up in a daze and her mother noticed that she was in a subdued mood when she opened her Christmas gifts and became worried for her. Her siblings, on the other hand, were whooping with joy when they unwrapped their presents and were constantly eating the nuts and oranges that had been put in their Christmas stockings.

During the day her listless behaviour continued to concern her mother, but around early evening, when the candles on the Yule tree were lit, she was relieved to see that Maggie's manner had changed. Instead of the deadpan expression she had been wearing since the morning she noticed a broad and contented smile appear on Maggie's face and wondered what had brought about this sudden change in her mood.

Maggie having overcome her initial shock to what had happened during the night had begun to realise the meaning of it. She no longer regretted carrying out the action and though she was worried that her mother might find the 'unopened present' a bit on the light side when she removed it from under the tree on Twelfth Night, she was glad that she had been able to let Charlotte finally get her Christmas present.

The Lost Carpet Bag

WHEN MOST OF the people of Great Britain were preoccupied with the siege of Mafeking in the Boer War, two brothers in the Derbyshire village of Little Longstone, by the names of Richard and Arthur Eatenton, were more concerned with their dislike and contempt for each other. Arthur was a hardworking and thrifty cobbler who had inherited the family business, and Richard was a feckless and unlikeable individual who was embittered that he had been left out of his father's will and had subsequently developed a violent hatred for his brother.

James Rawlings, a struggling landscape artist, became aware of the enmity between the two brothers when he regularly went to have his riding boots mended at Arthur's shop in the village and engaged in conversation with him. Arthur told him how Richard had been a wastrel who had caused nothing but problems to his late parents and had not deserved his share of the family estate. Rawlings had in fact known Richard Eatenton from his schooldays and knew him to be an obnoxious and cruel man who cared for nothing and nobody. As time passed by, Arthur became friends with James and confided in him about all the family secrets and James was shocked to hear of the levels of depravity which Richard had reached.

On one cold and damp November morning, James was

surprised to be asked to commit to a strange promise from Arthur. Arthur gave James a moth-eaten carpet bag and told James to keep it in a safe place and extracted from him a solemn undertaking never ever to let the carpet bag fall into the hands of his dastardly brother. James, not knowing its contents, was a little uncertain about taking the bag but was persuaded by Arthur's earnestness that it was the right thing to do.

Eighteen months after James had taken the bag and had put it under a false bottom in a wardrobe in the bedroom of the house he rented on Water Street in Bakewell, he was shocked to find out that Arthur had died in mysterious circumstances whilst walking through the woods near Monsal Dale on his way to visit a customer who was ill. His body had been found by a passing quarry worker and it appeared that Arthur had died of heart failure as there were no signs of injury on his body. A subsequent inquest concluded that he died of natural causes but there were several reports of a menacing stranger having been sighted in the area prior to his death.

On hearing of his friend's death, James took it upon himself to retrieve the carpet bag from its hiding place and find out the contents of it and finally solve the conundrum as to why Arthur had entrusted him with it. He tentatively took the brown mottled bag from where he had put it and pulled hard on the clasp that held it shut. The bag flew open and James was incredulous as to the sight that confronted him. He had never seen such a large amount of cash before and thought that the wads of five pound notes in the bag must have amounted to over ten thousand pounds at least. For a few minutes he was dumbstruck and could not fully understand the implications of what had occurred.

He had given his word to Arthur that he would, on no account, give the bag to Richard but he knew that he was morally bound to disclose the contents to the authorities and as Richard was next of kin to Arthur he was legally entitled to the money. Mental turmoil overtook him as he considered what course of action to take. He was two months behind with his rent and risked being evicted and his mother had a chronic illness and had no money to pay for the medicine she desperately needed. What was he to do? He had been brought up as a Christian and attended church every Sunday and knew that being honest and obeying the law of the land should be what he should do, but conflicting thoughts entered his mind and he wrestled with his conscience as he thought about the good he could do with the money he had discovered in the carpet bag.

After much consideration, he came to the conclusion that he had to be loyal to his dead friend's wishes and that he should not let the money fall into the hands of Richard who would no doubt use it for ill-gotten purposes. He realised that he had to be careful because if he started spending extravagantly people would wonder how he had acquired his money and he could find himself in trouble. After much thought, he decided that other than paying off his debts and supporting his sick mother he would not spend any of the money. This transpired to be a sagacious course of action, for within two weeks of Arthur's death James heard disturbing reports of Richard tearing Arthur's accommodation upside down in an attempt to find the missing carpet bag. Obviously Richard had somehow become cognisant that his brother had hidden a huge sum of money in a carpet bag, and he became even more alarmed when he overheard people talking in The Pack Horse in Little Longstone, saying

57

that Richard was mad with rage and would strangle with his bare hands the person who had purloined the bag.

Rumours spread rapidly that Richard Eatenton was becoming mentally unstable since his brother's death and this was partially due to the loss of the bag, for Richard wracked with debts from every direction, had counted on the money in it to save him from financial ruin. Swinging from rage to depression, Richard became a pitiful figure has he scoured the area looking for the elusive carpet bag. It was, therefore, not too much of a shock for the residents of Great Longstone and Little Longstone to read in the local paper that Richard had hanged himself on an ash tree near the hamlet of Rowland.

On finding out about the suicide, Rawlings had crisis of conscience for he realised that by the course of action he had taken he had greatly contributed to Richard's death. True, Richard was a despicable individual but he was still a human being and Rawlings, as a Christian, felt guilty for withholding from him the whereabouts of the carpet bag.

During the weeks after Richard's demise, Rawlings started to have disturbing nightmares and woke up from one of them when he thought he saw a dark spectre at the end of his bed. Furthermore, he started to hear footsteps behind him whenever he was walking on his own, and one particular night when he was walking on the riverbank in Bakewell he heard them again. He turned round abruptly and could clearly see a dark figure in the distance. This black apparition seemed to follow him everywhere and he decided to carry a knife with him as a precaution if the figure turned out to be a dangerous individual with criminal intent.

On one foggy evening in late October whist walking down Water Street on the way to his abode, he heard footsteps again and believed he heard some insulting words being said behind him. Frightened, he quickened his step and entered his home as fast as he could and locked the door with alacrity. Fearing that someone might have been in his house whilst he was out, he ran up the stairs to his bedroom to check that the carpet bag was still in its secret place in his wardrobe. He lay on the floor and was pleased to see that no one had touched it and the money was all there.

Just as he was closing the bag, he heard a footstep on the stairs and his heart started to thump in his chest as he wondered who it was. He fastened the wardrobe door and was just in the process of turning to face the bedroom door when he felt two strong hands grasp his neck and although he resisted fiercely he could not stop himself from being throttled. With his bloodshot eyeballs popping out of their sockets and an insufferable pain at the back of his head, he lost consciousness.

The Derbyshire Constabulary has, during the course of the last 150 years, had an exemplary record of solving murder cases and making sure that the perpetrators endured judicial execution or life imprisonment. However, the murder of James Rawlings by manual strangulation on the night of October 24th 1900, in Water Street, Bakewell, is still an unsolved crime and will probably always be so.

A Gothic Tryst

L IKE A PIECE of land that has been magically transplanted from Switzerland, the Derwent Valley around Matlock Bath seems to have the feel of another country and it's no surprise to discover that it has been visited by many famous personages over the centuries. One of these personages was Mary Wollstonecraft Shelley, author of the celebrated Gothic novel *Frankenstein*, and she must have been impressed with what she saw because a section of the novel concerning Baron Frankenstein's flight to England to escape the clutches of the monster he created, was set in the woods surrounding Matlock Bath.

Andrea Wilson was a young English Literature graduate from Sheffield and had, since her mid-teens, developed an interest in Gothic literature. She had read all the important novels of the genre but had a particular fascination for Mary Wollstonecraft Shelley's *Frankenstein* and had written a dissertation on it for her degree. Following graduation, she had hoped to find work in a publishing house specialising in horror and fantasy fiction but was disillusioned when she was turned down for all the positions she had applied for in this field of literature.

Running short of money and losing all hope of finding the job she wanted she reluctantly applied, like many other job-seeking graduate students, for a call centre position in a utilities company and was presently taken on as a customer advisor by an electricity supply company. After six months with the company, she was promoted to a senior customer advisor and became inured to the daily rants of disgruntled customers and desperate single mothers who had not enough money to pay their electricity bills.

On arriving home from work one evening to her sparsely decorated first-floor rented flat in Sheffield, she sat down on the wooden chair at her kitchen table and quietly wept. Surely, she had not spent three years at university to handle complaints from Mr and Mrs Average about their electricity supply. Surely, she should be talking to famous authors about their latest project and suggesting ideas to them that might be of use. It was baffling and depressing, and although she was on a reasonable salary and could live comfortably she decided that something had to change, and the first thing on her agenda was to find a boyfriend who had similar interests to her own and who could understand what she wanted from life.

Online dating, she realised, was the best way to achieve this objective. Of course, she thought, there would be lots of weirdos and deviants who would hit on her, but surely she would eventually find one decent guy who would share her love for Gothic fiction and who would believe in her and support her ambitions. Having shoulder-length dark brown hair and sparkling green eyes, she knew she would get plenty of male attention when she threw her hat into the online dating ring and, sure enough, when she did join a reputable dating site, the offers came flooding in.

Many of the men who contacted her were a lot older than her and, being as she had no intention of acquiring a sugar daddy, she dismissed them as unsuitable. Moreover, a lot of the suitors seemed suspiciously vague about their answers to her questions and she guessed they already had wives or girlfriends. The online dating caper was indeed a jungle with an abundance of predators and scavengers. Eventually, however, a really decent and good-looking guy made contact with her and he appeared to be everything that she had been searching for and they seemed very *sympatico*. His name was Mike and he lived in Derby. He was a project leader with a mobile phone company and he shared Andrea's passion for horror and fantasy fiction and also shared her taste in music. He had sandy coloured hair and was of medium height and looked, Andrea thought, like a young Harrison Ford.

Mike had attended the Whitby Gothic Weekend several times and sent Andrea a picture of him dressed as Count Dracula sitting on a stonewall near Whitby Abbey where, in Bram Stoker's novel, the evil Count had spent a night in a suicide's grave. Andrea had always wanted to go to the festival and was impressed with Mike's online accounts of his experiences there. After a couple of weeks of finding out more about each other and flirting online, they mutually decided that they should meet up for a first date and Andrea knew exactly where she wanted that initial date to be.

Matlock Bath was geographically in the middle of where they each lived and would be easily accessed by him by train from Derby and by her by bus from Sheffield. They both agreed that going by public transport was a good idea, for it would allow them to drink lots of alcohol and thoroughly enjoy themselves. Mike and Andrea both knew about the town's connection with the Frankenstein story and were eager to imbibe the special atmosphere of the place when they rendezvoused with each other there.

It was an early October Saturday morning when Andrea met Mike when he alighted from his train at Matlock Bath Station and they instantly felt a sense of elation when they saw each other for the first time. Oblivious to the other travellers, they hugged and kissed like lovers who had not seen each other for a long time, rather than, as they actually were, two people who were meeting up for the first time.

With the sun shining overhead, the town looked particularly beautiful with the trees in their autumnal red and golden attire, and Andrea and Mike strolled hand in hand through the town, blissfully unaware of anything but the woods that enclosed the town from both sides. Eventually, they stumbled into one of the town's drinking establishments and began to become moderately inebriated. After a couple of hours in the pub, they considered going on one of the town's cable cars to the Heights of Abraham but thought it would be more thrilling and more romantic to take a walk up the woods to the top of the valley. Andrea said they might even see a glimpse of Frankenstein's monster on the way up and teased Mike by saying she expected him to protect her if they did.

Finishing off their drinks, they left the pub and were instantly invigorated by the cold fresh air and bright sunlight that embraced them. Mike took Andrea's hand and led her into the woods and thought that when they went deeper into the arboreal maze it might be an ideal place for him and her to have their first passionate kiss. He became excited by the idea and gave her mischievous glances as they ascended together and she, in turn, returned them with interest. On finally reaching a place in the dark and brooding woods that seemed perfect for what he had in mind, Mike stopped and looked intensely at Andrea. Andrea intuitively knew what he wanted from her and began to feel her heartbeat increase as he put his arms around her. A warm flush went through her body as she felt his lips and tongue caress her as he pushed her backwards on to the trunk of a nearby tree.

The loving scene went on for a few minutes until, when looking over her partner's shoulder, Andrea noticed a movement in the woods. With Mike still embracing her, she was alarmed to see that the movement had been caused by a huge, dark-haired man looking maliciously at both of them. She let out a shriek and pushed Mike away from her and pointed in the direction of where the man was standing. "Look!" she exclaimed. "That man has been watching everything we have been doing; he's some sort of pervert or something."

Mike turned around and became enraged when he saw the tall and foreboding figure staring at him and Andrea. "Damn you, I'll teach you a lesson for this!" Not mindful of the fact that the staring stranger was far taller and far more muscular than him, he gallantly charged at the man and was surprised to see that the intruding voyeur ran away from him. Andrea shouted at him to come back, but his dander was up and she lost sight of him as he continued his pursuit in the woods.

After about ten minutes, Andrea became concerned that Mike had not returned to her and started calling for him at the top of her voice. The sound of her cries echoed all around the shadowy woods but no responding call came from Mike. Impatient with waiting and curious to find out where he was, she headed off in the direction he had taken in his chase. With daylight fading, she hesitantly began her search but became increasingly despondent when she could find no sign of him. When she had been trudging through the woods for a distance of about 400 yards, she heard the sound of a branch being snapped and turned in the direction from where it had come. Hoping that it was Mike making his return to her she was devastated to discover that instead of Mike's kind face looking at her it was the malignant face of the stranger that she saw.

A horrendous, primal scream escaped from her throat and she turned and fled in the direction of what she thought was the road below. She was running as fast as she could but she could hear the monstrous figure gaining ground on her with the sound of his clomping footsteps getting closer. In her rapid downward descent she stumbled several times but luckily just managed to save herself before she fell to the ground and became easy prey for her chaser.

Hope began to conquer fear as she heard the welcoming sound of passing traffic below, and she made up her mind in advance to run in front of any passing vehicle and wave her arms; hopefully, the car or lorry would have time to stop. She was sure she could make it when amazingly she saw a massive and ferocious dog running straight at her. She became mentally crushed when she realised that death was at the front of her as well as the rear.

Expecting the fierce dog to jump up and rip out her throat, she was relieved to see the canine run past her and head in the direction of her pursuer. The next thing she knew was falling into the arms of a man in a dark blue uniform and was merciful to find out that it was a police sergeant, talking to her and telling her to be calm as she was now out of harm's way.

A little while later, a female police constable informed her that her friend had been found in the woods with head injuries by a hiker, but told her not to worry as his injuries were not serious and he was expected to make a full recovery. As for the mysterious and sinister man who had been chasing her, she found out that he was a convicted murderer who had escaped from a prison near Derby three days ago. Looking to her left, Andrea breathed a mighty sigh of relief as saw her erstwhile pursuer, looking dishevelled and downhearted with blood pouring down his right arm where the police dog had bitten him, being led away to a waiting police car on the road below.

A Curious Winter Visitor

THE SNOW-COVERED OLD parsonage was an imposing and impressive sight in its position on a hill overlooking a congested churchyard full of Victorian gravestones that looked like soldiers on parade. Patrick Filbert, its owner-occupant, trudged along the snow on the way back from the railway station and fished for his keys in his pocket. It had been an arduous day at the engineering company he worked for and he longed for the sanctuary and comfort of his home where he lived alone after separating from his wife seven years ago.

The parsonage had become Patrick's oasis of calmness in his troubled and vexed life and he was glad he had enough money to buy it when it came onto the housing market. The church authorities had decided to sell the property due to falling attendances and the church services on Sunday were now given by a rector who lived twelve miles away in the town of Bowden. Other than Sunday, the church was closed to all visitors and during the week it looked somewhat forlorn and forsaken.

A gust of warm air met him as he pushed the front door open as he always arranged for the heating timer to activate the central heating an hour before he arrived home from work. He entered the large front room and was about to draw the curtains of its bay window when he noticed that there were footsteps in the snow immediately outside the window, as though somebody during the course of the day had been standing there and looking in. He thought it was strange because he seldom had visitors and he had not been expecting anyone to call on him that day.

He was annoyed that someone had had the effrontery to peep into his front room, and speculated it was either a nosey parker or a prospective burglar casing the place. At the weekend, he decided, he would acquire CCTV equipment and install it immediately so that in the future he could check up on anybody intruding on his property when he was at work. However, he was fatigued from his day's strenuous and taxing labours and did not want to think about the matter anymore. Taking off his coat, he went straight to the kitchen to prepare his simple but much needed evening meal.

After devouring the margarita pizza and chips he had put in the oven to cook, he sat down with a glass of Piesporter wine and turned the television on so he could listen to the evening news and weather forecast. The news mainly concerned the continuing Arctic blast that had enveloped Britain for the last eight days and the weather presenter predicted that following another snowstorm tomorrow the temperatures would drop to record lows. The weather outlook was very unwelcome news to him because, as he was a manager, he was duty-bound to attend his firm's annual Christmas party tomorrow evening and it would mean that there would be travel problems for him afterwards. Hopefully, he thought, the trains would still keep running and he would be able to get home alright.

An hour and a half later, after he had watched a documentary on satellite television about the battle of Gettysburg in the American Civil War, he retired to bed and whilst reclining in bed he reflected that he was lucky that he was part of a generation that had not had to suffer the horror and trauma of fighting in wars like the one he had just viewed on television. Also, just before he dropped off to sleep, apprehensions came upon him about the forthcoming work's Christmas party. He was not really a gregarious person and always looked on the annual party as something he endured rather than enjoyed. Hopefully, he comforted himself, his workmates would not get too drunk and it would pass off reasonably well and without any embarrassing incidents.

He had been asleep for over two hours when he was jolted out of it by the loud banging of somebody knocking frantically on his front door. He looked at the time on his alarm clock and was unnerved by seeing it was only three o'clock in the morning. Anybody, he thought, who wanted urgently to contact him at this hour of the night would have first rang him on his mobile phone. Primal blood started to flow through his veins when he realised that the person who had knocked violently on the door could attempt to break in, and he hurriedly reached for the cricket bat that he kept under his bed for circumstances just as this and, carrying the bat, he went downstairs to check who was at the front door. He also made sure he carried on him his mobile phone so that he could ring 999 for the police if things escalated.

He first looked out of the front window to see if he could see the suspicious caller but was disappointed to find out that he could see nobody. From there he went to the front door and tentatively opened it and was again disappointed to find no one there. Looking out at the snow-covered scene, he was both surprised and alarmed to discover that the caller had left no footprints in the snow. Either, he concluded, he had imagined the violent hammering on his front door or he had been visited by a phantom. Closing and bolting the door, he returned to his bedroom and tried to reason out what had occurred but was still totally perplexed when sleep overcame him.

The electric alarm rang at 6.30am and he rose out of bed immediately and went downstairs to check that everything was alright. He noticed that he had left his cricket bat by the front door and again contemplated what had happened. However, he had a busy day ahead of him and could not spare the time for any more reflection. After having toast and coffee, he rushed out of the house to make for the railway station and get on board the early morning commuter train. Walking briskly through the snow-drenched churchyard, his attention was drawn to a headstone that was totally devoid of any snow and stood out from the rest for this reason. Maybe, he thought, it was a freak of the wind and weather but he did not have the time to investigate and hurried off to catch his train.

When he was on the train, rather than read his customary detective novel to pass the time, he dwelt again on what had happened the previous night but he could not, for the life of him, fathom it out and eventually gave up trying. Looking out of the carriage window, he watched the predicted huge snowstorm dump its load on the already snow-covered countryside and hoped that there would be no problem getting back home in the evening. If the weather forecast was correct the snow would stop falling by the afternoon and a severe frost would then take place. Noticing an intrepid jackdaw flying in the sky, he felt sorry for all the wildlife that had to endure the rigours of the winter and for those that perished because of it.

On reaching his office station, he assiduously completed his workload for he knew that by lunchtime everyone would be in a party mood and no work would then be possible. Every year was the same and he was uneasy in his mind about the shenanigans which would inevitably take place. He was always amazed how his married work colleagues behaved at the Christmas party compared to the ones without partners, and it seemed to him that Christmas was used by many people as an excuse for debauchery and infidelity.

Sure enough, as in all previous years he had worked there, people stopped working at around noon and beer and wine bottles miraculously appeared. Later on, they all headed for the hotel where the Christmas meal and party had been booked and Filbert did his best to go with the festive flow but he didn't really enjoy these raucous occasions. He did, however, enjoy the traditional turkey dinner and mildly flirted with some of his female work colleagues and joined in a communal dance with several of them. All the members of staff of the firm were in a frivolous and happy mood and were cavorting and laughing with each other to such an extent that they were oblivious to the severity of the weather outside. At around 10pm, Filbert felt he had been at the revelry long enough and said his goodbyes and wished everyone a merry Christmas before heading for the railway station to catch the last train to his home town.

Noticing at once the severe cold that stung his face when he left the ornate Victorian hotel where his work's party continued at full steam, he hoped that the train could get through and was not snowbound somewhere. He had imbibed far too many alcoholic drinks and swayed from side to side as he walked through the deep snow to the city's main railway station. Breathing a sigh of relief, he saw the welcome sight of the train waiting to leave the station and quickly hopped on board and collapsed on a seat next to the carriage entrance. Opposite him was another reveller who looked the worse for wear and had obviously drunk too much as well.

The warmth of the railway carriage made Filbert fall asleep and he had to be shaken out of it by the train's conductor when they reached his destination, which was the end of the line. Dazed, he staggered out of the carriage and took his bearings before he headed home. Floundering in the snow, he realised that the snow had fallen much heavier here than in the city and it appeared to be much colder. He had about a mile and a half to walk and he began to realise it would be difficult to do in these conditions and, in addition, the amount of alcohol he had imbibed and the depth of the snow he was walking through caused him to stumble and fall regularly and he began to lose items of clothing and personal effects. His route home started to resemble that of a retreating army with lots of impedimenta strewn behind it and, unbeknown to him, he had already lost his woollen hat, gloves, mobile phone, wallet and, most important of all, his house keys.

Combined with losing items of clothing and the intense cold of the night, he began to shiver violently and show signs of mental confusion. His journey home, which in good weather he could do in less than twenty minutes, began to feel like an endurance test and he started to fear for his life. The lure of his centrally heated home, however, spurred him on but he was becoming increasingly frozen and fatigued. Finally, the graveyard came into sight and he cut across it using the headstones to help him keep upright. Resembling a prize fighter who was wobbly on his feet after receiving a devastating right hook, he staggered to the front door of the old parsonage and put his frozen and unwieldy hand into his pocket to retrieve his house keys. An incredulous look crossed his face, followed immediately by one of sheer terror, as he realised he had lost his keys on the route from the train station and crumpled to his knees in total despair.

Soon he found himself prostrate on the ground and he knew that the insidious and dangerous effects of hypothermia were kicking in. The temptation to just lie there in the snow and fall into deep sleep was huge but he knew that if he allowed himself the dubious luxury of this it would be a sleep that would lead to his oblivion. It would be a sleep of death and he used his last resources to fight it and decided to try and use his mobile phone to call for help. As he was fumbling in his pocket for the device he noticed, from the corner of his eye, a tall, dark figure approaching from the churchyard that appeared to be wearing a top hat. The figure, whoever he was, passed by him and miraculously opened the front door. He then retraced his steps and went behind Filbert and lifted him up by his arms and dragged him into the hallway of the former parsonage. Having done this, he unceremoniously vacated the premises and closed the door behind him and, presumably, Filbert thought, headed back to where he had come from. Filbert could feel the comfort of heating straight away and knew that he could now safely allow himself the luxury of drifting off into a deep sleep. A sleep which he felt assuredly he would definitely awake from.

Six hours later, with a throbbing headache and an accompanying feeling of nausea, he was awoken by the sound of the postman pushing a fistful of Christmas cards through his letterbox. Even with all the symptoms of a bad hangover he was relieved he was still alive and reached in his pocket for his mobile phone so he could find out the time and discover how long he had been sleeping in the hallway. He became startled when he realised that not only had he lost his house keys but he had also lost his phone and a cold sweat instantly enveloped his body. The stark truth dawned on him that if it had not been for the mysterious appearance of the dark-clad stranger, the postman, who had just delivered his Christmas mail, would have discovered his frozen corpse lying outside his front door.

The Man On The Walkway

I N THE TWILIGHT years of the twentieth century, it was decided by many nations and communities that some worthy project should be undertaken to mark the approaching new millennium. Indeed, many people thought that the advent of the year 2000 was of such important historical, religious and social significance that it could not come and go without a great deal of fuss being made about it. One such town that decided to mark the occasion with a notable project was New Mills in the north-west region of Derbyshire.

After much discussion, they decided to construct a 'Millennium Walkway' which would allow the Torrs gritstone gorge to be made passable to walkers. After diligent planning and ingenious engineering, the walkway was completed in 1999 and was more than ready to welcome in the second millennium.

Stan Hobbes, a widower and retired sweet factory worker, was initially against the project but after ten years of taking his morning constitutional across the impressive walkway in all the four seasons of the year, he had changed his mind. At six feet tall and still with a full head of hair, even though it was all grey, he proudly and happily walked across the structure every day.

As is the way with many older citizens, they first curse

a new invention or change of method which they think is the preserve of the young, so much so that they appear to be hardened misoneists. However, after a few rebellious years they finally succumb to the charms of the new-fangled device, building, method or whatever, and begin to embrace it. Yes, Stan accepted that the walkway project had been a good idea after all, and no more so than on one particular early winter cold but stimulating morning, as he stood in the middle of the walkway and watched a heron, perched on a stone on the edge of the fast flowing River Goyt below him, waiting patiently for a fish to catch.

The last few months had been very stressful and traumatic for Stan, and he cherished the solace that his early morning outings across the walkway gave him, for he had been in a permanent state of despondency since the day he received the results of all the medical tests that had been carried out on him. His general practitioner had told him, in as positive a way as possible, that he was in the early stages of Alzheimer's and had reassured him that new drugs were available that could arrest the development of the disease and that he should not go away from the surgery completely down at heart.

Looking again at the regal and ever patient heron, the words "completely down at heart" echoed in Stan's mind. If anything, he reflected, he had been absolutely down at heart during the past six months and felt himself denuded of all hope. Kicking away the fallen autumn leaves in front of him, which resembled giant cornflakes due to the previous night's keen frost, he dwelled on the forthcoming Christmas. It might, he ruminated, be the last Christmas he would experience any cognisance of the fact that it was that time of the year that Christians celebrated the birth of

Christ. Indeed, in the future, would he be in cognisance of anything? The changing seasons of the year had always been appreciated and loved by him but would they, too, become meaningless to the man he would soon become.

As he was wallowing in his self-pity, he suddenly became aware of a movement in the derelict Torr Vale Mill that stood directly opposite the walkway. He thought he saw a man, a very old man, darting from one window to the next and staring directly and accusingly at him. The man had protruding eyes and grey stubble and seemed to be in a very bemused state. Stan was aghast at what he saw and could not comprehend what was happening, for he knew the window where the man was looking at him had no floor under it where an individual could stand and look out. Indeed, the mill, at that particular section, was a hollowed out shell and the floors of the building had collapsed decades ago. Either, he thought, he was looking at the ghost of an old mill worker or his Alzheimer's was beginning to kick in and he was at a loss to decide which one it was.

Hoping and praying that it was actually a ghost that he was seeing, he playfully surmised that it could be the restless spirit of a Victorian weaver who, after being too old to work at the mill anymore, had been forced to enter the local workhouse. He indulged in his musings further and felt that it was probably a man who had had no relatives who would look after him and, after finishing work, he had no means or savings to avoid him seeking the dubious charms of the workhouse.

People mistakenly think, Stan thought, that the horrid workhouses of yesteryear were full of feckless and idle fellows and women of easy virtue, but the truth of the matter was that they were full of old men and women who, like knackered horses, were not fit for work anymore. He remembered reading Jack London's *The People of the Abyss* as a young man and recalled his description of the sad and decrepit old people who inhabited those awful places. In those days, he further reflected, old age was something to be feared by the working class; there was no old-age pension until 1909 and anyone without money was a hostage to fate.

Yes, he sympathised with the apparition and could very much understand why he looked so disconsolate and miserable. It must indeed have been terrible to have been old and poor in those 'good old days', he sarcastically remarked to himself. But was he not in a similar situation to that tragic ghost who was ogling him? True, he had a good pension and had no money worries and a nice home to live in but what good were these to him if his condition drastically worsened? He had no relatives to care for him or, more correctly, wanted to care for him, and although he would not have to dread the workhouse he was not at all that happy about having to enter its modern day equivalent: the residential care home. Disappearing as mysteriously as he had appeared, the ghost of the old mill worker could no longer be seen by Stan and he continued with his walk after he had satisfactorily noted that the watchful heron had finally managed to catch a fish.

That evening after he had listened to an episode of *The Archers* on the radio, he poured himself a glass of German beer, sat back in his favourite leather armchair and took stock of his situation and what he had seen, or thought he had seen, on the walkway that particular morning. He thought it was strange how old age affected people in different ways, and saw it as unfair that some people with active and alert brains suffer terrible physical deterioration and some older people who are physically fit and in good shape, like himself, suffer terrible mental deterioration.

Looking at the picture of his dead wife, Dorothy, on the mantelpiece, Stan pondered whether the old man on the walkway had been a widower as well. Furthermore, did he not have any sons or daughters who were prepared to look after him? Is that why he looked so pitiful and despairing? In thinking about the mysterious man in the mill he considered he was not in such a different situation than him. Sure enough, he had a son, David, an engineering graduate, who did not live that far away in Sale, South Manchester. But he could not see his son's wife, Susan, a maths teacher at a community school in Cheshire, allowing his son to give him a home in their household. Yes, he thought, there wasn't that much difference for his future than there had been for the old man on the walkway in the past.

After taking another sip of beer Stan grinned and spoke aloud: "*Plus ça change*," and started to remember old friends of his who had died over the preceding years. Like many people, he had almost felt a sense of invulnerability and superiority that he had managed to live to a good age whilst others he had known had died young or comparatively young. Now, with the knowledge that he was a sufferer of Alzheimer's, that sense of arrogance had disappeared; he considered that maybe his old friends, who had died quickly and unknowingly, might have been the lucky ones after all.

Fear of the unknown is one of the worst fears that men and women can have, and there is nothing more unknown than what a person thinks and feels when he enters the latter stages of the accursed disease that he had been recently diagnosed with. True, physicians could see the outward signs but they could only speculate about what the victims actually experienced. Thinking of his beloved dead wife, he felt happy that she would not be there to witness his illness develop and he felt proud of himself that he had not taken up with another woman since Dorothy had passed away.

As a practising Christian, he had always thought it a paradox that his Church had allowed widowers and widows to remarry in church. Surely, if there was life after death there would be an embarrassing situation in heaven when the bereaved spouse died, and then had to explain to their first wife or husband about the other partner they had promised to honour and obey. It was a conundrum and Stan could not reason it out; he was glad that it was puzzle he would not have to get involved with when he died.

Before retiring to bed, Stan made his customary look through his front-room window to check on the state of things outside and noted, even though it was not yet December, that one of his neighbours across the street had put a Christmas tree up in his window which was duly glistening with blue lights. Stan, on seeing this, shook his head and pined for the time when people only put up their decorations a week or two before Christmas.

The next morning saw another severe frost and Stan wondered whether if it was a wise thing to do to take his usual morning stroll along the Torrs. However, after having his customary breakfast of toast and marmalade washed down with a cup of Darjeeling tea, he cast off any worries of slipping or catching a cold and made ready to go on his ritual, daily walk. He was also curious to see if he would see another glimpse of the pitiful old man at the mill again.

Quickly descending the steps that led to the gorge, he headed straight towards the Millennium Walkway and when he was halfway across he scanned the derelict mill intently to see if he could see any sign of the old man's ghost. Yet, although he looked at every one of the Torr Vale Mill's hollowed windows he could find no trace of him. Perhaps, he thought, it was a chance sighting of the spectre he had seen yesterday and it might be that he would probably never see him again.

All of a sudden, he became aware of a voice on the walkway and he immediately turned away from looking at the mill and was astonished to see the old man standing about thirty yards ahead of him on the structure. Instantly, he became concerned and felt his heart thumping away under his overcoat. He wasn't sure whether to turn back the way he had come and go back home or bravely advance to get a closer look at the disturbing apparition.

He heard what resembled a moaning sound and decided to face his fears and walk in the direction of the old man who was staring directly at him with a vacant expression. As he approached the ghost, Stan became painfully aware of just how ugly, decrepit and repulsive the old man was and noticed that he was dripping saliva from his lower lip and had deep creases all over his countenance. Moreover, his pallor was a sickly yellow, which reminded Stan of the colour of an old and rotten banana, and when he was less than ten yards from the man he was shocked to see that the spectre had started to walk towards him and became very nervous about what would happen.

When the ghost was within six feet of him a very disturbing thought crossed Stan's mind: was this really a spectre or was it a *premonition enfantine* of what he would become, due to his affliction, in five or ten years' time? At this thought, a searing pain crossed his chest and he found himself having difficulty breathing, and then he felt his legs go weak and he lost consciousness as he crashed to the floor of the walkway.

Three weeks later, a strong wind blew an errant newspaper into the path of a middle-aged married couple out walking their dog along the Torrs Gorge. The woman picked it up and immediately recognised the picture on the front page of it as the distinguished and friendly old man who, until recently, they had regularly seen on their walks in the gorge. She passed the paper to her husband and he read aloud what was printed under the picture of the man: 'It has been concluded by the local police, after detailed enquiries and a post mortem, that Stan Hobbes, aged 74, who was found dead on the Millennium Walkway on the morning of November 29th, died from natural causes. At first the police thought that his death was suspicious and an investigation had been launched. However, a police spokesperson confirmed yesterday that no further enquiries would be made and Mr Hobbes' body could be released for burial.'

The Last Christmas Dinner

THE CONDEMNED PRISONER thought that the snow-covered fir trees he saw out of his railway carriage window looked like giants with hoods as the steam train travelled at speed through the Hungarian countryside. Arpad Dodog, a young carpenter, had been found guilty of murdering his love rival at the Pécs regional court and was being transported to Budapest so that he could be executed by the pole method of hanging used in the Austro-Hungarian Empire.

The date of his execution had been set for 8pm on December 29th 1906, and the train had left Pécs station at 9pm in the evening of December 23rd so that Arpad could be installed in the main prison in Budapest before the Christmas celebrations began on the 24th. Accompanying him on his lugubrious journey were two armed prison warders who were grim, formidable and taciturn as they sat on either side of him. He had been handcuffed to the more ferocious looking one and resented that he could not move his hands freely on his fateful journey. He had tried to engage them in conversation but they answered him with one- or two-word answers and seemed reluctant to converse with him. Giving up on them, he took refuge in his own thoughts and the snow he saw falling outside reminded him of his winter childhood in rural Hungary.

Arpad's parents had a smallholding and Arpad and his six brothers and sisters helped them with all the chores around the farmhouse. Arpad was good with his hands and used to help mend the wooden fences which penned in the livestock. Winter was always a harsh time for the family, but Christmas became a magical time and the children forgot their hardships and looked forward to the appearance of the festive tree on Christmas Eve. Their parents always managed to store away little treats for them and, like magicians, they managed to find lots of delicious nibbles for the children to eat when the tree was dressed.

The thought of those Christmas treats brought Arpad out of his reverie, and, contrasting then with now, he realised he would probably only get cold pork and tepid cabbage for his last Christmas meal in his condemned cell. Moreover, he would only be given cold water to drink with it and for dessert he would be lucky if he was given dry, insipid and hard biscuits. It was depressing for him to think of his last Christmas on this earth and he cursed himself for letting anger and jealousy get the better of him. However, he sadly realised that the actions one took in life could not be reversed and that he would have to suffer the consequences. Death did not scare him but the thought of missing out on the joys of life distressed him. When he remembered his dead mother's smile he became unmanned and quietly wept as the train carried him to his doom; he was happy that the two prison guards did not see his discomfiture.

Whilst he was thinking of yesteryear, he noticed that the train started to jolt on the tracks and without any warning he and the two guards were thrown forward as the engine driver slammed on the brakes. Within seconds of hearing the brakes screeching, a sound like an explosion was heard and the carriages of the train rolled over and over again, and, in what seemed like a ride on a chaotic carousel, he was thrown all over the place. The carriage came to rest on its side and Arpad's forehead was badly cut as he landed on one of the broken carriage windows. With moaning and whimpering sounds coming from injured passengers, he clambered to his feet and noticed that the two prison guards had been knocked unconscious by the collision. He rifled through the pockets of the prostrate warder who he had been handcuffed to and quickly found the key to unlock his cuffs, and then noticed that a gaping hole had been made in the roof of the carriage in the crash by which he could make his escape.

He rushed to the hole and as he came out the other side he was met by an icy blast of wind with snowflakes falling all around him. Whilst the stricken railway engine was making sounds that resembled those of a dying dragon, he ran to the nearby woods and decided he would go as deep into the forest as he possibly could. He counselled to himself that the further he could get away from the crash scene the better. Five minutes earlier he could not have imagined that he would ever regain his freedom again, and although he was not properly attired for the cold weather he was euphoric about having the opportunity to escape his fate.

He had trudged through the snow for about three hours when he realised that his physical condition was weakening. He was frozen to the bone and he realised that if he did not reach shelter soon he would die much sooner than 8pm on December 29th. Moreover, he heard the howling of a wolf pack in the distance and knew that the wolves would soon pick up his scent and look on him as bountiful prey.

Staggering on through the forest, he was amazed to see

a light in the distance and used all his remaining strength to head in the direction of its source. As he came nearer, he realised that the light was emanating from a peasant's hut and his spirits rose as he began to whiff the scent of wood smoke coming from the hut's chimney. Realising he had to come up with a plausible story when he knocked on the hut's door, he decided to say that he was a woodsman whose aged horse had had a seizure due to the cold weather and had collapsed, causing the cart he was riding on to topple over. This would account for the nasty gash on his forehead, which had been caused by the train crash, and would allay the suspicions of the inhabitants of the hut.

Thumping robustly on the door he anxiously waited for it to open, and, after what seemed an interminable wait, it creaked ajar and an old man with a grey beard looked at him with trepidation. Arpad recited his fabricated tale and was pleased to see that the old man believed him and invited him into the hut. Entering, he was overcome with relief when he felt the heat coming from the fireplace and collapsed on the floor in front of it from cold and fatigue, and from out of nowhere a stout middle-aged woman rushed to him and cradled his head in her arms.

"Blankets, blankets, hot soup!" cried the woman, and a handful of young children ran in all directions and within minutes he was covered in woollen blankets and was being spoon-fed hot paprika-flavoured soup by the caring woman. Feeling drowsy after eating the much needed soup, he was helped to a corner of the room by the old man and fell quickly into a deep sleep.

When Arpad awoke, it was early in the afternoon of Christmas Eve and he was surprised to see that five cherubic-looking children, three girls and two boys, were looking at him with intense curiosity. Smiling gently in their direction, he was pleased to see that they all smiled back at him as he heard a woman's voice encouraging them to get their coats on and follow her out to collect firewood for the forthcoming Holy Night. The dark-haired woman, presumably the mother of the children, also smiled at him and pointed in the direction of the old man standing next to the fireplace, who, she told Arpad, would look after him until she returned from her chore. Swiftly, she and her five children trooped out of the hut and left him alone with the kindly but rough-featured man.

Asking him if he felt alright, the old man put some logs on the fire and when Arpad told him he was feeling fine he asked him if he would help with decorating the Christmas tree. Arpad instinctively knew what the procedure was and felt honoured to partake in the family ritual. In Hungary, the Christmas tree is only decorated on Christmas Eve and the children must not be present when the tree is dressed; they are always taken out of the house on some pretext to allow this to take place. Hungarian children, unlike children in Britain and America, believe that baby Jesus (*Jesuska*) and not Santa Claus, brings them their presents.

Arpad helped the old man put tinsel, candles, gingerbread and handmade ornaments on the tree. Most importantly, he hung *szaloncukor* on the tree, a Christmas candy covered with chocolate and wrapped in silver, gold and red shiny paper tied with bows. Guests are always welcome to take them from the tree. Finally, he helped carry in all the neatly wrapped Christmas presents for the children and placed them carefully at the base of the tree. Arpad felt privileged to be a part of the ceremony and memories of his own Christmases came flooding back to him and filled him with joy.

When darkness came outside, the old man lit the candles on the tree and everything was ready for Holy Night. Soon afterwards, Arpad heard the excited cries of the children and couldn't wait to see their faces when they came in and saw the magical tree. Barging in, they were astounded by what they saw and stood for a few seconds in wondrous amazement at the beautiful Christmas tree. Their mother told them that they would have to help her prepare the Holy meal before they could open their presents and they obediently followed her into the kitchen. The youngest of the girls, who went by the name of Magdi, hesitated before she left the room and took one of the *szaloncukors* off the tree and with a broad smile gave it to Arpad before skipping off to join her siblings. Arpad carefully unwrapped the sweet, putting the shiny paper covering in his trouser pocket, and savoured it as it dissolved in his mouth.

With delicious fried fish smells coming from the kitchen, Arpad sat down in an armchair and sipped red wine from a tumbler, which the old man had given him. When the children had done all the kitchen chores, they were ushered in front of the Christmas tree and sang the lovely Christmas carol 'Angel from Heaven', which brought happy tears to Arpad as he thought of his lost childhood. When the children spread straw under the dinner table, to represent the Bethlehem stable where Jesus had been born, Arpad knew that the Christmas feast was about to begin.

Fish soup was brought in first, which Arpad eagerly dipped his bread roll in. After the soup came the traditional sumptuous fried carp and boiled potatoes. Arpad never enjoyed a meal as much as the one he was partaking in and could never have believed a day ago that he could have done so. For dessert the *beigli* walnut pastry rolls were brought in and Arpad teased the children by throwing the poppy seeds from the beigli at them. Merriment was in abounds and as he imbibed glass after glass of wine, Arpad felt like an honoured guest.

All goods things must come to an end and Arpad, drowsy through drink, was shown to his bed in a back quarter of the hut. As soon as his head hit the pillow he fell asleep and many dulcet dreams came to him as he slumbered. In one of the dreams he imagined that one of the children was tickling his chin and blowing his hair and when he turned over he was shocked to feel that he was shaking with cold. When he opened his eyes, he was horrified to see not one of the children tickling him but a police bloodhound licking his face. Aggressive voices demanded he get up and Arpad was shocked to see five armed policemen surrounding him. One of the policemen grabbed his hands and put a heavy pair of handcuffs on him and told him to walk with them.

As he was taken to the nearest town with a jail, he looked back and was incredulous to see that the hut had disappeared and all he saw was the burnt and weather-beaten foundations of an old building. He asked the nearest guard what had happened to the building and was brusquely told that a fire had ripped through the hut twenty years before and all the family that had lived in it had perished. Arpad felt a cold shock go through his body and bowed his head in disbelief as he was led away.

Twenty-four hours later, he was incarcerated in his condemned cell in Budapest's main prison and sank to his knees in utter despondency. He made a silent prayer and reached in his trouser pocket for a handkerchief to wipe the tears from his eyes. However, instead of a handkerchief he felt some paper and as he took it out of his pocket he noticed that it was coloured gold, silver and red, and became elated at what he saw. His tears dried up immediately and an enormous smile came to his face as he stood up and clenched his fists. He punched his fists time and time again in the air and, by so doing, demonstrated to the watching warders that he had no fear whatsoever as to his upcoming fate.

The Missing Allotmenteer

THE LARGE COUNCIL allotment site was overlooked by a hillock which had been a prehistoric burial site. The hillock had many mature trees on it and was nicknamed by the local people as 'Skeleton Wood'.

When Linda and Geoff Hooper visited the site for the first time, they were impressed with the setting of it and on a cold but sunny late winter day they were taken aback by its tranquillity and beauty. They decided immediately to take the tenancy of the allotment plot that they had been offered and looked forward to turning it into a productive allotment once again.

The only thing that slightly affected their decision was the strange fact that the allotment had not been occupied for over ten years. There seemed nothing wrong with the site; it had good drainage and top soil and had a good aspect as far as the sun was concerned. The couple were completely mystified as to why it had not been snapped up before and were also perplexed by the apparent long list of people who had declined the option of taking it on.

Linda began to draw up plans for how the allotment would look and had visions of being feted for turning the derelict site around. In her imaginings she would be awarded prizes by horticultural societies and be the toast of the allotment world. The couple had decided that it would become their grand project and they would commit lots of their time and money to its realisation. Both of them had retired early from their jobs and had been looking for something to occupy their time.

Geoff had retired from the engineering firm he worked for when he was fifty-nine and Linda had retired from her job as a betting shop manager when she was fifty-six. Whereas he looked much older than fifty nine, she, on the contrary, looked much younger than her age and could have been taken for being in her mid-forties. Moreover, with her blonde-dyed hair, she was still very attractive and received lots of admiration and attention from men of all ages.

Their attention, however, was always rebuffed for she was still very much in love with her husband of thirty-five years and was content to be a loyal and dutiful wife. Geoff, on the other hand, had a straying eye and had, unbeknown to his wife, many secret affairs over the course of their marriage. His unassuming and diffident veneer was a good camouflage for his philanderings, and his wife had never suspected that he had many dalliances over the course of their matrimonial life.

Linda set about transforming the forsaken allotment by, first of all, clearing all the empty and discarded half bottles of brandy and whisky that had been left there by the itinerant tramps who had used the allotment site during the summer. George, the doyen and self-appointed leader of the allotment site, had told her that there were two tramps who had been using her plot over the last few years. One of them was nicknamed by the allotmenteers as 'Billy Bighead', on account of his oversized head. George told her that he was a friendly and amicable tramp who had been using the empty sheds of the unused allotment site for years. He was partial to brandy and that accounted for all the empty brandy bottles that she had found. The second tramp, he warned her, was a different kettle of fish altogether.

He was nicknamed by the allotment holders as 'The Black Fox' because of his mop of dark hair, and was a very nasty piece of work indeed, and if she took his advice she should have nothing to do with him whatsoever. "Many prize bantams had gone missing on account of him," George angrily informed her and shook his head in disgust. "Empty whisky bottles," he advised her, "are the sure sign he has been hanging around your plot and many of the people around here suspect he had something to do with Ron's…" He abruptly stopped talking and Linda felt as though he was annoyed that he had mentioned the name "Ron".

George finished the conversation with Linda by saying that she would only see the vagrants in the summertime as they tended to go to the cities when the weather became colder. "In winter," he continued, "the countryside is a very cold place and in the big towns and cities there are more places to stay warm."

Linda and Geoff decided that when the two tramps came back in the summer they would find a completely new vista awaiting them. Every day they worked like beavers digging and turning over the ground, which was covered in weeds such as ground elder, horsetail and bindweed, and pulling down the old sheds and erecting new ones. During their work they were amazed to find large quantities of lime and soot in the soil. They found out from the internet that the lime had been used by previous tenants to make the ground better for cabbages and cauliflowers to grow. The soot, they also found out, was put on the soil by former tenants to warm the ground up and encourage the vegetables to grow.

Linda remembered from her childhood days her father coming home with cabbage seedlings, which he had bought from the local market for six for a shilling. She decided that she and her husband would specialise in brassicas and asked her spouse to repair an old and very large Second World War cold frame in the allotment plot for this purpose.

The Second World War had been the golden period for allotments with the 'Dig for Victory' campaign encouraging people to open plots. Indeed, by the end of the war the number of plots had risen to a staggering one and a half million. Sadly, after the war had ended the demand for plots reduced considerably; the rising prosperity and falling food prices of the 1950s and 1960s had lessened the demand for plots and the pastime went into decline. However, from the 1970s onwards there had been a renaissance in the British tradition, and Linda and her husband were, in their work on their plot, flying the flag for the movement.

Geoff did an excellent job on renovating the cold frame, and some of the other plot holders asked him for assistance in repairing their dilapidated ones as well. One of these was an Italian widow in her early fifties who had carried on working her plot alone when her husband had died in a car crash three years ago. She was called Sonia and she made regular visits to the Hooper's allotment and invariably asked Geoff for some advice or help with her own plot. Linda did not mind because she liked working on her own and appreciated the communal and helpful spirit of her husband in giving aid to a fellow allotmenteer. Sonia in return gave useful tips to both of them and showed them where everything was on the allotment complex. Indeed, she even showed Geoff around Skeleton Wood and pointed out to him where the prehistoric barrow was.

As the months passed by, the project started to take shape and no one would have recognised the now renovated site from the dilapidated one that existed less than three months before. There was a new greenhouse and two new sheds, which both had two water butts next to them. The vegetable plots were neatly bordered with flagstones, and sparkling new garden tools and a wheelbarrow ornamented the lovely allotment. With the onset of spring and warm weather, Linda and her husband would sip wine together and look over the allotment with a feeling of pride and joy. It was how they had envisaged it would be when they first visited the abandoned-looking site and made plans to resurrect it from its mysterious neglect.

The only problem was that the balmy nights when the couple sipped wine together started to become a rarity. It seemed to Linda that Geoff was always helping Sonia out or he had to do some favour for an old friend. Although she liked the solitude she also liked talking with her husband about the development of the plot. Moreover, when it became twilight she felt a little uneasy on her own in the allotment and always made sure her mobile phone was close at hand if any unwanted or unsavoury visitors arrived.

The allotment started to yield some produce and Linda was thrilled to pull up some radishes that she would use in a salad. It was on one particular sunny afternoon that she was doing this when she discovered, to her alarm, an empty whisky bottle amongst the plentiful radishes. She and husband never drank whisky and she was both mystified and nervous about who had put it there.

Like many allotment sites there had always been problems with local teenagers, and petty theft and vandalism were not uncommon. Indeed, she and her husband had been warned about this by the other allotmenteers when they took on the plot. However, she had not witnessed any gangs of teenagers drinking or larking about and came to the reluctant conclusion that it was the tramp that went by the sobriquet The Black Fox who had deposited it there.

Linda looked on it as similar to a home invasion and was very angry and concerned about it. She rang her husband immediately and asked him to come to the site at once. Geoff, who had been helping Sonia repair her greenhouse, came to Linda's side within minutes. When her husband arrived she raised her voice and said, "The audacity of it, the bloody audacity of it. We put new fencing all around our allotment and it is obvious to anybody that is occupied and cultivated. It's a bloody cheek." She vehemently continued her tirade to her husband by saying that the tramp had no right to trespass on the plot. She added that there were plenty of empty and unused allotments and he could have entertained himself in those.

Linda's husband agreed totally with his wife and was annoyed that the tramp had smashed down some of the new fencing that he had recently and painstakingly put up. He said to Linda that he would repair the damage but thought that the tramp would be wanton enough to break in again and would consult Sonia about what to do. She, he thought, would probably have had experience of intruders and might give the couple some good advice about what to do with the unwanted visitor.

It actually transpired that Sonia had had no problems with intruders in her many years as an allotmenteer and it appeared that the tramp who was nicknamed the Black Fox, seemed only to be interested in using Linda and Geoff's plot as his impromptu drinking and sleeping domain. Apparently, she informed Geoff, the previous tenant, who was called Ron Brindley, had given him permission to use the allotment when he had nowhere else to go. This came as a big and unwelcome surprise to Linda's husband, especially as this tramp had been considered by the police as the main suspect in the mysterious disappearance of Mr Brindley twelve years ago.

Linda looked aghast at her husband as he informed her about what Sonia had told him and stomped her feet on the ground and exclaimed, "That's why the allotment had been unoccupied for so many years. Everybody knew its bad history except us. We were the bloody mugs who accepted the tenancy." Her husband quietly nodded his head in agreement and went on to tell her more about what Sonia had said.

Since he was last seeing working on his allotment on a hot and sultry July night twelve years ago, no trace or sighting of Ron Brindley had been seen since. Apparently, so Sonia said, the whole allotment had been dug up by the police and the forensic department had scoured the other allotments looking for clues to his disappearance. However, nothing was ever found and as time went by the police spent less and less time on the case.

Many of the allotmenteers thought that foul play had taken place and wanted the police to treat it as a murder inquiry. Ron, they argued, was a creature of routine and a very stable and conservative individual; it was very unlikely that he had just boarded a bus or train and gone walkabout. No, the consensus was that something bad had happened to him and The Black Fox was the likely culprit. The police, indeed, must have thought the same because they repeatedly brought him in for questioning but could not charge him because no proof could be found to link him with the missing person.

Linda stood flabbergasted at what she had just heard and felt angry that no one had the decency to tell them about the history of the allotment before. She was grateful for what Sonia had told her husband but wished she had informed him earlier. It occurred to Linda that if she and her husband had known about the former tenant's disappearance they might not have taken on the tenancy of the allotment. It was very possible, she darkly thought, that a murderer was lurking about their precious plot.

She contacted the council's Parks and Open Spaces Officer, Peter Wharton, about the situation and she also made a complaint to the police. A police community support officer came round to see her and her husband and seemed very sympathetic to their situation. He commented that the trespassing tramp, The Black Fox, whose real name he informed them was Terry Richardson, had been a nuisance on the allotment site for many years and he had indeed been treated as a suspect in the unexplained disappearance of Ronald Brindley.

The robust officer divulged to them that Richardson had served as a soldier in Bosnia and what he had seen happen there had seriously disturbed him. Apparently, his character completely changed for the worse, and he became an alcoholic with a propensity for violence. He reassured them that he would keep an eye on the situation and have a word with Terry Richardson when he next encountered him.

Later, when the council officer rang Linda about the intruder, she remonstrated with him that she and her husband should have been told about the allotment's previous history before they were offered the tenancy. He officiously replied that it was not the council's policy to inform new tenants about details concerning past tenants as this would have been a breach of confidentiality. She disdainfully ended the phone call and made a pact with herself that when she met the horrid tramp she would give him a piece of her mind.

Several weeks passed before any evidence of the malignant tramp invading the allotment was seen again, and when it occurred it both sickened and infuriated Linda. On a hot, sunny and windless afternoon, she had been putting a large clump of comfrey plants, which were all over the allotment site and which she had just recently pulled up, into the allotment's compost holder when she saw a large group of flies hovering just behind it. She gingerly edged forward and was shocked to see that the object of the insect's interest was, unmistakably, human excreta with a horde of flies crawling all over it. Moreover, a discarded whisky bottle was lying on the grass six feet away and there could be no doubt that Richardson had invaded the sanctity of their allotment again. She shouted at the top of her voice, "Bastard!" and ran to Sonia's allotment where Geoff was helping Sonia to earth up her potatoes.

Two days later, when Linda went unusually early to the allotment at half past six in the morning to build a wigwam support for her runner beans, she hazarded to see the so called Black Fox scampering over the allotment's perimeter fence. It was the first time that she had actually seen the villain and instantly her dander was up. She raced towards him brandishing a Dutch hoe and harangued him with all the foul language she could think of. Surprisingly, he remained silent and did not answer her back and walked slowly off in the direction of Skeleton Wood. It appeared,

Linda thought, as though he was completely oblivious to the abuse she had hurled at him.

Whereas the black-haired and darkly-clothed vagabond appeared to be calm and collected, Linda, by contrast, was a bag of nerves. Quivering inside and out, she ran to the opposite end of the allotment and tried to call her husband on her mobile. However, because her hands were trembling uncontrollably, she couldn't manage to enact it and had to sit down on the grass for a few minutes to compose herself. Eventually, she had calmed down enough to allow her fingers to make the call to her husband and she gave him a brisk rundown of what had happened and pleaded with him to come to the allotment, as fast as he could, because she feared the tramp might return after the vitriol she had shouted at him.

Whilst she waited for her husband to appear, she poured herself a coffee from the steel thermos flask she had brought with her and attempted to eat the cheese and tomato sandwich she had made that morning. Just within her sight she noticed a movement in the grass surrounding the cabbage patch and started to shake violently thinking it was the execrable tramp. She breathed a sigh of relief when she discovered it was one of the many rats that infested all the allotment plots and turned round to resume eating her al fresco breakfast.

Sipping the warm aromatic coffee and admiring the beautiful morning, she was completely unaware of the D-handled and full sized digging spade being swung behind her. The reverse side of the blade smashed into the back of her head and she instantly crumpled to the ground like a cow that had been stunned by a captive bolt in a slaughter-house.

The jostling, which her body started to receive, brought her back to a state of semi-consciousness and she sensed that she was being transported on what appeared to be a wheelbarrow. Her whole body ached and she had a tremendous headache but she could apprise that her arms and legs had been bound and she was trussed up like a dead chicken. It seemed to her that she was being pushed uphill but she could not see anything because a tarpaulin cover was wrapped around her.

After what seemed like an interminable journey over rough ground, the wheelbarrow came to a sudden halt and she could just make out a hand lifting up the cover and was thankful to see the clear blue sky again. A few seconds later, she sensed the wheelbarrow tilting upwards and then she experienced the sensation of falling, with her body rebounding on the hard sides of a deep cavern or lime kiln. Finally, she came to rest on the bottom and there was just enough daylight coming from the surface for her to view something touching her. She shuddered with terror when she realised it was a human skeleton clothed in what appeared to be an old man's time battered cloth cap and blue overalls.

Three Seconds

DEEPER AND DEEPER went the two lovers into the Stygian forest as they purposefully sought to get as far away from the sights and sounds of other people as they could. Every twenty yards they advanced through the bramble-covered undergrowth, they turned round to check that they were not being followed, for Aquilina and Paulus Benitus were fugitives from Roman justice and were worried that someone had seen them enter Pan's kingdom and informed the authorities.

Paulus, a handsome dark-haired tribune, had been a favourite of the British governor Clodius Albinus who had been tricked in to believing he would be the successor to the emperor Septimus Severus. However, when Severus had defeated his main rival he had reneged on his promise and Albinus, furious with this betrayal, had crossed the channel with an army from Britain to confront Severus at Lyon in 197AD. The result of the battle was a complete victory for Severus, and Albinus and his army were wiped out. Paulus Benitus, who had fought valiantly but vainly at the battle, just managed to escape with his life and fled back across the channel and took refuge in the northern town of Aquae Arnemetiae.

Whilst he licked his mental and physical wounds at the holiday town, he met a young Roman-British woman by the name of Aquilina, who was working as an attendant at the *mansio* he was staying at. She was a raven-haired and voluptuous beauty, and when she first gave him a beautiful dimpled smile whilst waiting upon him at his dining table he fell instantly and hopelessly in love with her, and it proved to be nothing resembling an unrequited love, for Aquilina returned his love with interest and they soon found it difficult and discomforting to be apart from each other for any length of time.

Aquilina had come to Aquae Arnemetiae from the town of Durnovaria in the south-west of Britain when the owner of the *mansio* she worked at there had decided to try his hand at running one in the north of the province, for he had been told that many famous Roman patricians and legionaries visited Arnemetiae when they were stationed at Eboracum. Indeed, the great Hadrian had visited the town when he toured the province in the early part of the second century because it was nearer for him to take the waters there than Aquae Sulis in the south of the province.

When she first settled in the town she was unhappy because it was much colder than Durnovaria, but she soon became used to the northern climate and grew to love the town for it was surrounded by beautiful forested hills and valleys where she went for long walks when the weather was temperate. When she and Paulus became lovers, she introduced him to all the secret places she had discovered and took him there for secret little meals at all times of the year, where they would dance together to the sound of blackbirds singing in the daylight and owls hooting in the moonlight. Paulus had never known any woman with the beauty and charisma of Aquilina and couldn't envisage his life without her being part of it and she felt the same way about him.

After several months of happiness and bliss in the town, their idyll was brutally shattered by the news that an investigatory magistrate had been sent by Severus to the town to seek out the rebels who had opposed him. Paulus knew that he was high on the list of the wanted and considered fleeing the town but he could not contemplate leaving without his beloved Aquilina accompanying him. However, he realised that her going with him would put her at considerable risk of being accused of aiding and abetting a fugitive from imperial justice. Time was not on his side as he considered his options, and very soon a detachment of legionary soldiers placed him under house arrest as the magistrate awaited orders from Severus.

Paulus, who was under no illusions what his ultimate fate would be, knew it would only be a matter of time before he was put to death and decided to take matters literally in his own hands and fall on his own sword as an honorary Roman, but he was deeply mortified at leaving his adorable Aquilina behind him and feared that she could be tortured for being the consort of a rebel leader. After telling her what he planned to do she hugged him tightly and vowed to go wherever he went, even if that meant returning to her ancestors considerably earlier than she had expected. Paulus tried to talk her out of that course of action but knew in his heart that though it was horrible it was the most expedient thing to do.

Aquilina informed him that there was a secret passage out of the cellar of the building that would enable them to avoid the guarding soldiers and escape over the walls to the secluded woods that surrounded the town. Moreover, when they had reached a certain distance into the forest, she told him that they would drink a glass of wine together and make love to one another for the last time before Paulus thrust his sword into his heart. She promised him that three seconds after he had taken his life she would take a potion given to her by the druids that would kill her instantly and they would die in each other's arms, and she pledged to him that she would return to him in another body at a designated time in the future where he, in turn, would be in a different form. The druids had preached to her that true love could conquer death and instructed her that if she fervently believed that then it would come to pass and they would be reunited in the future.

It was a cold and miserable February day in the town of Stockport in North West England when Elizabeth Winterbottom decided that she had enough of shopping In Marks and Spencer's and Debenhams and was going to take the earliest bus she could back to Buxton where she had made her home after moving from Dorset in the south-west of the country. She saw the red bus she wanted to catch barely thirty yards ahead of her when it drove away just has she started to sprint to catch it. "Three seconds, three bloody seconds," she shouted to herself as passers-by wondered who she was speaking to.

Dismayed that she would have to wait in the freezing cold for another thirty minutes for the next bus, she cursed her luck and thought that she had been born under an unlucky star for nothing ever seemed to go smoothly for her. Stamping her feet in exasperation, she decided to kill time by looking at her Facebook timeline and considered putting a status update on it about how things never went right for her. In what seemed an eternity, her bus eventually arrived ten minutes late and she gave the bus driver a sardonic smirk as she bought her ticket and then took her seat halfway down the aisle.

Stopping and starting through the heavy traffic, the bus came to an abrupt stop outside a hospital and a dark-haired, enigmatic-looking man entered the bus and took his seat opposite Elizabeth who gave him a friendly but restrained smile. As the bus continued its erratic progress through the outskirts of Stockport, Elizabeth gave him surreptitious glances and was sure that she had seen him somewhere else before but could not for the life of her think where. Moreover, she had a strong intuition that she knew him from an earlier period of her life. She went through a quick and random check of all the schools, colleges, workplaces and holiday destinations she had been to but could not fathom out where she had known him before. Perhaps, she mused, he looked like someone she had been friends with her at some time and that was why she thought he was familiar.

As the bus entered the countryside of Derbyshire, Elizabeth became aware that the mysterious stranger was making furtive glances in her direction and was obviously attracted to her. She mulled whether to make eye contact with him as she watched the sheep grazing in the fields through the window of the bus.

Indeed, the stranger was struck by her looks and was patiently waiting his chance to strike up a conversation with her, for he was very impressed by her shining dark hair and her elegantly rotund physique. Moreover, he noticed that when she saw something out of the window that pleased her she had a lovely dimpled smile that would melt the heart of any man.

When the bus was within a few miles of Buxton, Elizabeth felt the need to stand up and stretch her legs and this gave the admiring stranger the opportunity he had been waiting for to engage her in conversation. "Yes," he agreed, "it's easy to get pins and needles in these uncomfortable bus seats."

Slightly startled by his comment, she hesitated for a moment as to whether to reply but then thought that he seemed an interesting and handsome man and smiled and said, "I know, I'll catch the train next time I go to Stockport."

They developed an instant rapport and Elizabeth found out that the stranger's name was Paul Benet who had come to stay in Buxton to get away from the hustle and bustle of London where he had fallen foul of a heinous clique in the political party of which he had been a member. Elizabeth remarked to Paul that she was sure she had met him before some years ago and Paul, in turn, stated that Elizabeth also looked familiar to him but he could not for the life of him think of the place where he had seen her before.

After they left the bus at the same stop on Buxton's market place, Paul asked Elizabeth if she would like to accompany him for a drink in one of the pubs called the Sun Inn and Elizabeth eagerly accepted the offer. It was the start of a romantic friendship, and as the weeks passed they found out more and more about each other and were delighted to discover that they had lots of things in common. Both, for example, were interested in politics and current affairs and they also shared a love of nature and wildlife. Moreover, the two of them shared a love for all things historical and Paul was impressed to hear that near to where Elizabeth lived on Park Road, just a little way up from the Leewood Hotel, was the former home of Vera Brittain, the author of

Testament of Youth. Indeed, opposite her erstwhile home was a Victorian pillar box and both of them mused that Vera most probably posted love letters in that very box to her fiancé, Roland. Furthermore, a few houses up from where Vera lived was the birthplace of Robert Stevenson, the director of the iconic film *Mary Poppins*, and Elizabeth would mischievously parody the film with her umbrella when they passed the Rockwood residence.

After several months of going out together, Paul and Elizabeth had shown a Victorian patience in waiting to consummate their relationship, but Elizabeth had decided that the time was right to put the seal on the relationship and suggested that that they have a picnic deep in the woods that surrounded a nineteenth-century folly, nicknamed 'Solomon's Temple' by the locals. Duly they entered the secluded woods on a hot May afternoon armed with rucksacks full of food and the accoutrements of eating outside, and made their way steadily into the deepest part of the arboreal labyrinth.

Eventually they came to a flattened area, which they both decided was ideal for holding an al fresco repast, and began to quickly unpack the blankets and food ready for the forest feast. However, as they were unpacking, something came over both of them and rather than continue preparing the picnic they started to become aroused and immediately engaged in a passionate tumble which had only one logical end.

Unbeknown to Elizabeth and Paul was the solemn fact that just two feet under the ground where they were making love for the first time, were the earthly remains of two Roman lovers who had committed suicide centuries before. Their bodies had never been discovered and their bones had been covered by more than a thousand years of autumn leaf fall, and as the frantic lovemaking of Elizabeth and Paul shook the soft ground which held the skeletons of Aquilina and Paulus, it could be concluded that the druids who had supplied the deadly potion to Aquilina had been telling her the truth in their prophecy.